Pauline King

Christine's Career

A Story for Girls

Pauline King

Christine's Career
A Story for Girls

ISBN/EAN: 9783337062750

Printed in Europe, USA, Canada, Australia, Japan

Cover: Foto ©Andreas Hilbeck / pixelio.de

More available books at **www.hansebooks.com**

CHRISTINE'S CAREER

A STORY FOR GIRLS

BY
PAULINE KING

ILLUSTRATED

NEW YORK
D. APPLETON AND COMPANY
1896

THIS VOLUME IS LOVINGLY DEDICATED TO

CHRISTOPHER, CORNELIA, AND MERRITT.

CONTENTS.

LIST OF ILLUSTRATIONS.

CHRISTINE'S CAREER.

CHAPTER I.

THE COTTAGE AT VERVERNEY.

HE Seine is a wonderful river with its wind-ings and twisting through meadows, fields, and cities down to Paris and the sea. It sees many quaint and curious sights in all its travels, but nowhere is it more beautiful than at Ververney, where it passes under the old crumbling gray bridge.

Ververney is only a little mouldering market town now, but it was a thriving Norman city once, in the days when the beautiful half-ruined cathedral, the graceful spires of which are to be seen for miles around, was new. When the quaint, bulging fronted houses, that line the narrow streets, settled quite off the perpendicular in the centuries since they were builded, were the homes of stout burghers and men-at-arms.

Once a week, on market days, the town breaks out

1

into great excitement—peasants with baskets of fruit and vegetables, venders of poultry and cattle, and peddlers of quaint Norman pottery, bargain and scream themselves hoarse for a few hours. The rest of the time the town sleeps away its existence, and flocks of pigeons fly about the streets undisturbed save by the evening chimes.

Up from the river valley rise gently sloping hills, divided off into neat garden patches and trim vineyards, with each carefully pruned vine twined in an orderly manner around a green stake. Nestling in among the gardens and vineyards are dotted clusters of dwellings. Over the tops of the high stone walls, with which every little holding is surrounded, one catches sight of small one-story stucco cottages coloured pink or green or blue, which the sun and rain of many years have transformed into beautiful hues. And there are glimpses of gay flower gardens and of old gnarled orchard trees through the iron gateways.

Straight up the long hill about two miles from Ververney there is such a cluster of little houses, which wear a more prosperous air than most of those in the neighbourhood. Once upon a time, indeed, and not

so many years ago, it was as unkempt and forlorn as
any of its neighbours, and then, so the story goes, a
great artist wandering down from Paris stopped there
and found the place beautiful, and, staying there to
paint, he bought one of the little cottages, and lived
in it for many years. Thus the fame of the beauty of
Ververney spread, and many artists came, and they,
too, settled down in the little pink and blue cottages,
until the place was full of French and English.and
American families.

In one of these gardens on a warm August afternoon a girl of some twelve years was lying in the shade
of an apple tree reading a book. She was quite flat on
the grass, with her feet kicking in the air, and her short
red hair tumbled about her face in disorder. She was
so absorbed in her book—and indeed how could it be
otherwise, for she is reading Little Women for the first
time?—that though we enter the garden she will not
raise her head, but goes on reading, her chin in her
hands, quite oblivious even of the ripe mulberry bushes
hanging with luscious fruit, which are well within her
reach.

The gate opens and shuts, but she heeds it not; then

suddenly a gruff but kindly voice, speaking in the Norman *patois*, breaks the stillness.

" Mademoiselle! Mademoiselle! help me, dear child; the dinner of Monsieur will assuredly be late. The market was truly so fascinating that it was impossible to tear one's self away, and already it is close to the hour when Monsieur will return."

The speaker was a little, bent old woman whose wrinkled and weather-worn face was surrounded by a spotless white cap with wide flapping sides, the head-dress of the peasants in that part of the country. She wore also the customary sack and short blue petticoat, the latter displaying a great pair of wooden shoes, and strapped over her back was a big willow pannier out of which stuck the ends of the various purchases she had been making in the town.

Christine sprang up from the grass, dropping Little Women in haste. As she stood aiding the old woman to unstrap her load one could see that she was rather tall for her age, and her face, now that the mass of heavy locks was pushed away from it, was, though in no wise regularly beautiful, a sweet, girlish one, lit with a pair of intelligent hazel eyes.

"Mademoiselle! help me, dear child."

Christine deftly unfastened the straps of the pannier, listening while the good woman displayed her bargains, each one of which had been secured only by her remarkable sagacity in beating down the price sou after sou. The old woman's economical foibles and her ancient enemies in the market were well known to Christine.

"You need not worry about being late," she said, answering the servant's self-reproaches at being so long delayed. "It's such a clear evening I fancy father will stop to finish the sunset by the brook, so dinner would have to be late anyway." She spoke quickly in French, speaking it as though it were her mother tongue, with an accent very different from the old woman's nasal *patois*.

"Ah, mademoiselle, if you will only spread the table for me, everything else I can attend to." And she carried the heavy basket into the small tiled kitchen which glistened with an array of burnished copper utensils.

While 'Toinette, called "Bon femme" in affection by the little girl, was bustling about in the kitchen, lighting the stove and muttering ejaculations of horror at the lateness of the hour, accompanied by many twitchings of the immaculate cap, Christine had tied a big apron over her pretty short-waisted muslin and was piling dishes upon a tray with a skilfulness which argued that this was not the first time the market of Ververney had proved attractive to 'Toinette.

" Forget not the salad plates, nor the bowl of mayonnaise, mademoiselle," called 'Toinette, breathlessly puffing at the bellows to light the charcoal stove. " Also——"

But Christine, not heeding, was out of the door and down the garden path, carrying the big tray with its glistening array of glass and china. On she went to the spacious vine-covered arbour at the end of the garden, for, strange as it may appear to boys and girls who regard eating in the open air as a picnic, it is the custom in France, with rich and poor alike, to dine and even breakfast out of doors in fair weather.

There was a big table in the arbour, and Christine took a linen cloth out of the drawer and set it with a great bowl of roses in the centre, a dish of crisp green lettuce at one side and a tall Venetian flagon of " vin du pays " just as she knew her father liked to see it.

Then she went down to the gate to watch for the first glimpse of her father coming down the flat road. The peasants going home from their work in the fields nodded " bon soir " as they passed, to the little wistful face pressed against the bars. The last gleam of their white caps faded out of sight and the road was quite quiet, but still her father did not come.

" Bon femme," she cried at last, " I am going down to fetch papa; he must have forgotten how late it is, and he will be very hungry."

The big iron gate slammed behind her and she sped down the road in the direction of the brook where she knew her father was painting. There, sure enough, he was sitting in front of his easel with his big palette on his thumb and his great sketching box at his feet.

" Ah! here comes my little dinner bell," Mr. Averil called gaily as he caught sight of the little figure with its flying curls tearing along through the meadow.

Christine snatched a hurried kiss, keeping clear of his great sheaf of wet brushes and the large palette, terrible destroyer of muslin gowns. Then she looked at his sketch of the evening sky, the willow trees, and the water radiant with the many-hued reflections of the setting sun.

"Such a beautiful picture, papa!" she said, which was her invariable comment upon every sketch, for she thought everything that her father said or did was absolutely perfect. "Isn't it most done? Wouldn't you like some dinner?"

Mr. Averil laughed, scraping up his palette and picking up his sketching things.

"Yes, dear, quite done." The father and daughter spoke in English. "I was just going home when I saw my Will-o'-the-wisp coming after me." He packed up the wet sketch and, shouldering the load, they left the meadow, walking home slowly through the clear twilight which lasts so long abroad.

For all the years Mr. Averil had lived abroad, one would never have mistaken him for anything but an American, and although Christine was born in France and had never seen her own country, she had the unmistakable stamp of an American girl.

Christine's mother died when she was a tiny baby, and the father and daughter were all in all to each other.

In the winter they live in Paris, and Mr. Averil paints in the big studio, while Christine went to school in the "Rue des petits enfants." In the summer they come down to Ververney, where they own one of the picturesque cottages, and Christine lives out of doors from morning until night.

The big paint box has to be put away and Christine's rough locks put in order before they can sit down to dinner; but finally she is seated opposite her father at the table in the arbour with a steaming bowl of appetizing bouillon before her.

"And what has my little girl been doing all this afternoon? It was market day, was it not, and you were alone?"

"Oh, yes. Bon femme went to market."

"And was delayed, I suppose." For it is a standing joke that Bon femme never, never can understand where the time goes on market day.

"Oh, yes, and I set the table; does it look quite right?"

"Quite right, my little daughter," looking over the tasteful table. "You have certainly improved since the first time; you are getting to be quite a house-

2

keeper. It didn't take you all the afternoon to accomplish such perfection, did it?"

"Oh, no, papa, certainly not; I did lots of other things. I had a beautiful drive with Cherie."

Now Cherie—which in French is about the equivalent for darling—had been, when first given to Christine, a soft and amiable young donkey who quite answered to the description of his name. With years Cherie, however, had grown stiff and cranky, but he was still in his mistress's eyes the most beautiful steed in the world, and she was never happier than when, seated in her little tan-coloured cart, she was urging him off a walk or trying to persuade him that meals of thistles at all hours were not a bit good for his digestion.

The idea of anybody having a beautiful drive with Cherie struck Mr. Averil as rather a remarkable feat; but Christine went on recounting her adventures:

"Then when Cherie got tired of going he just turned around and came home, and I read all the afternoon. I had a new book called Little Women—such a lovely story—one of the——"

But Christine broke off suddenly; her spoon remained suspended in the air as she gazed in astonishment over her father's shoulder. Mr. Averil turned his head and was no less surprised than his daughter. A lady with severe features and gray hair, her tall figure clad in black, was coming up the garden path. She had a strange foreign air quite different from any one Christine had seen before, and, as she stood hesitating which way to turn among the rows of hollyhocks and dahlias, her stiff black figure looked like a veritable bad fairy godmother to Christine, and she felt quite stony when the unknown lady, catching sight of the inhabitants of the arbour, turned that way.

"Why, Georgie," cried Mr. Averil, recovering from his astonishment and advancing enthusiastically to meet the stranger with outstretched hands, "what a wonderful surprise! Christine, dear, this is your Aunt Georgiana."

Another moment and she realized that the lady's face, for all its stern features, was most sweet and kindly. She was folded in the stranger's arms, and a soft, gentle voice said pleasantly:

"My dear little niece, how glad I am to see you!"

Of course Christine had always known that she had

an Aunt Georgiana away off in America. Several times
a year she wrote English letters to her in her little
cramped French hand, and at Christmas and on birth-
days she always received some pretty gift from across
the sea, with a few short messages of love and congratu-
lation. But this distant aunt had never seemed like a
real person to her, and America and everything con-
nected with it was so hazy in her mind that she could
not have been more surprised if her relative had announced that she had just arrived from the moon.

"I meant to send you word I was coming, Christopher," said Aunt Georgie, "but I am such a poor
sailor that I was afraid I might not come at the last
moment. Some friends of mine were coming over, and
I joined them, though my trip can only be a flying one.
I was absolutely wearying for a sight of my little niece."

Bon femme, all excited by the new arrival, bustled
out of the cottage with an extra plate, knife, and fork,
laying a place for "Madame," with many apologies lest
the soup should be cold.

Aunt Georgie did not look a bit like a bad fairy
when she took off her bonnet, showing a smooth, broad
forehead and soft gray hair waved away from a straight

parting. Her eyes were so friendly that Christine, though too shy to speak, could not help thinking that she was an especially nice aunt.

She seated herself at the table and tried Bon femme's excellent soup, her quick eyes taking in the dainty arrangements of the table, the pretty garden, and the vine-covered house which was bathed in the last rays of the setting sun.

" This is absolutely Arcadia, Christopher," she said. " I don't wonder people like to live abroad when they can find such a charming place as this. I am sure if I staid here any length of time I should never be able to tear myself away from a pale-green house and such excellent dinners in a picturesque arbour."

Christine sat listening. She wondered what colour the houses were in America, and why her aunt thought it picturesque to have dinner in the arbour.

CHAPTER II

HRISTINE never forgot that meal as long as she lived. Although she is now a woman, she can shut her eyes and see the arbour and the dinner table, her father sitting opposite her and her aunt's erect figure against the background of vine leaves. She was quite awed by the stranger's arrival, for though she was such a chatterbox when she was alone with her father or Bon femme, she was always very shy with other grown-up people.

Aunt Georgie evidently understood the nature of little girls and the excellence of the motto that they should " be seen and not heard," for, her affectionate greeting being over, she devoted herself to conversing with Mr. Averil about America and people and things of which Christine had never heard before. Now and then she would smile pleasantly at her little niece or glance affectionately at her with her dark eyes, so that

Christine's shyness began to wear off, and with the appearance of dessert—a great bowl of strawberries and a pitcher of yellow cream—she found voice to hazard the remark which had been hovering on her lips for some time.

"Perhaps you are tired and would like a cup of tea, madame," not quite knowing whether to say aunt or not. "Shall I go and make it?"

"Aunt—not madame," said the lady, and it was surprising how, when she spoke, her thin face was lit by such a lovely smile that no one would ever have thought her a bit severe. "But do you know how to make tea, dear?"

"Oh, yes," said Mr. Averil, putting his arm lovingly around his daughter, for she had slipped from her chair. "Christine is my tea-maker, home-maker, and all—you can trust to her making it just right. Bon femme considers tea a medicine to be taken after much boiling in case of severe illness, so an English lady showed Christine just how to make it. She is very careful to heat the pot and have the water boiling just as she should."

Christine turned to go to the house, but before

she got quite out of earshot she heard her aunt say:

"What a big girl she is for her age, and what a nice little maiden! Is she talented? She looks interesting."

Christine heard the remark and immediately quickened her pace. She did not care to hear her father's reply. It was the one blot on an otherwise happy childhood that people always would say when they saw her for the first time, "Well, my dear, are you going to be an artist like your father? I fancy you will be having a great career one of these days." Then Christine would blush and hang her head, for, truth to tell, she showed not the slightest symptom of inheriting either her father's talents for painting or the genius of her young mother, who, when only eighteen, had modelled a statue so beautiful that the French Government had bought it and placed it in the Luxembourg Garden.

Most of the time—for Christine was a healthy, normal child—her mind was filled with childlike things, but now and then the strange lack of talents in one who by right should have had them made her think seriously, and the question of what the career that was expected of her could possibly be, puzzled her extremely.

In a little while she came back to the arbour bearing a steaming pot of good strong tea which was very refreshing to her aunt after the hot journey down from Paris. The grown people were still interested in talking of matters with which she had no concern, so she went out into the garden and sat down on the ground under her favourite tree. She wondered what America was like and if she would ever go there; and if the boys and girls all had such a good time as they had in Little Women, one of the few American stories that she had read. She was sure that she would like her new relative ever so much, and she only hoped that her aunt would like her as well and not be disappointed at the dearth of those talents about lack of which she was herself so much concerned.

"Dear, dear!" thought the child, "if only a fairy would come along and say to me, 'Dear Christine, what would you like to have?' I would just answer, 'Oh, a talent, fairy, anything at all, I don't care what, but a nice big talent so that people won't be disappointed in me.'"

Her meditations were just then broken in upon by a click of the garden gate and an apparition appeared which, while it could certainly have never been a fairy, presented in the dim light something of the appearance of an elf—a girl in the shortest of short blue petticoats with thin, lathlike legs stuck into big wooden shoes, and her thin, angular body so closely squeezed into garments that she had evidently outgrown that the big flapping white cap which she wore on her head gave her the appearance of a mushroom on a thin stalk. She entered the gate holding by a halter a mild and chastened-looking beast which proved to be Christine's donkey Cherie, sorrow for his wicked conduct in running away being imprinted upon his downcast head and hypocritical countenance.

In the winter when the Averils were in Paris Cherie was left in charge of one of the peasant families, and it was characteristic of the amiable animal that whatever place he really belonged in, he was always anxious to return to the other by fair means or foul.

"Oh, Celeste!" cried Christine, recognising the quaint figure as a denizen of this earth, "where did you catch him? How could he have got out? Oh, you naughty, naughty Cherie! I must have left the gate unlatched when I went down to the brook to call papa to dinner, and you must have got out of the shed then. It is strange he did not stop to eat up our flowers," for the donkey usually left a trail of destruction behind him. " I hope he did not eat up any one's garden."

" No, indeed, mademoiselle, he has done no damage," answered Celeste, tying the donkey's halter to the apple tree so he could graze contentedly. " When we were at supper we were suddenly startled by hearing him bray, and there he was with his head stuck over the garden gate as though saying ' Bon soir! ' "

" Sit down, Celeste," said Christine hospitably, "and have some mulberries; that bush is just full of ripe ones."

"*Merci*, mademoiselle! " and Celeste, seating herself on the turf, stretched out her hand for the luscious fruit. " Mademoiselle is too kind," she said in her polite French way.

Although she was only a few years older than Christine, and much smaller, she had the air of being a little wise old woman as she sat munching the mulberries— Celeste, " la petite blanchisseuse " she was called. Indeed, so early do the French children learn to help in the house and fields that when a mere toddler she had taken charge of the soap at her mother's side when washing in the Seine. During the past winter all sorts of misfortunes had come knocking at their cottage door, and her mother, after a long lingering illness, had died. Then Celeste had bravely taken her place at the washing trough and had washed and ironed, fluted and starched, with the nimblest fingers.

Christine, who had seen Celeste every summer since she was born, was further attached to her because of her devotion to Cherie despite his eccentricities, and she was glad to have the girl take a quiet hour's rest from the hot kitchen in which she was always at work when she was not carrying great baskets of clean linen home.

"My aunt has come to see me from America," said Christine, for, after the manner of French peasants, Celeste would not speak to one her superior in station unless spoken to.

"Your aunt, mademoiselle, the sister of monsieur?"

"No, mamma's sister; and, oh! she looks so nice."

"You must not let her carry you home with her,"

said Celeste, for, in common with many of the other peasant girls, the advent of Christine each spring with her bright face and kind ways was an event in their workaday lives.

" No, indeed, how could she take me with her? I would never leave father, and I'm sure he would never go away from Paris. Perhaps some time we may go for a little while, but I've never thought of it."

The two girls talked on of little events and interests. Celeste's capacity for mulberries seemed unlimited, and Christine did not hurry her until their conversation was interrupted by hearing Mr. Averil calling,

" Christine! Christine! Where are you? We must be going in. See, the moon is coming up over the wall and it is quite late."

" In a moment, papa," she answered. " I must put Cherie back in his stall," and having, with Celeste's aid, secured the animal in the little stable and closed the garden gate after polite " bon soirs " and courtesies from her white-capped guest, she joined her father and aunt in the drawing-room.

Bon femme had gone to bed long ago to be ready

to rise at dawn in thrifty French peasant style, but she had lighted the candles in their brass sconces so that the big room which served as half studio, half drawing-room, looked most picturesque in the dim light with its big piano, the tapestry-hung walls, and bits of choice bric-a-brac

"What a beautiful room!" said Aunt Georgiana, settling into a comfortable chair. "But, Christopher, does Christine always have late dinners with you and sit up so late?"

"I was wondering," laughed Mr. Averil, "if our odd arrangements did not rather surprise you. Yes, Christine always had her little bowl of milk with me when she was quite a baby. We were all the family, you see, and I didn't want the child to be lonely. You may have noticed that she by no means ate a dinner to-night; she has her supper with me, that's all. She usually goes to bed at nine, but to-night she knows she can have an extra half hour on your account."

Just then Christine came in and curled up in a corner of a big comfortable-looking divan that was covered with soft pillows.

" Won't you play for me, Christine? " said Aunt Georgie, wishing to draw the little girl out.

There was a trying moment while Mr. Averil said that Christine's music had been given up because the little girl had absolutely no ear. And then he sat down to the piano and played Chopin's and Schumann's beautiful music, which he had played to Christine ever since she was a baby and were like her cradle songs.

Soon it was time to take Aunt Georgiana up to the inn for the night, as the little cottage could in no wise be stretched to accommodate a guest. So the big lantern was lighted, for there are no street lamps in little French towns, and Christine tripped on ahead with it while Aunt Georgiana followed on Mr. Averil's arm. Truth to tell, Aunt Georgiana had never spent such an amusing evening before—the dinner in the arbour, the music, wandering through the high-walled lanes escorted by a child carrying a lantern—it was like the things people did in books, and she wondered what her correct Boston friends would think if they could see her.

Christine banged on the wooden gates of the inn · courtyard, calling " Cordon! " The *concierge* pulled

the gates open from some mysterious distance, and
Aunt Georgiana disappeared.

Then Christine and her father hurried home, for it
was far, far past her usual bedtime.

As Mr. Averil kissed her good-night he said quietly:

"You have not been unhappy alone with father?"

"No, no, indeed."

"Nor missed having other children to play with?"

Christine drew herself up a little.

"You have not been lonely without any grown-up
people, but just me, have you?"

"No, indeed, dear little daughter."

Christine wondered why he spoke so sadly, as though
their good time together was at an end. Perhaps Aunt
Georgiana was coming to live with them, she thought;
and indeed on the following day, when her father went
up to the inn and had a long talk with her aunt, Christine decided that it must be so. She wondered how
such a very particular-looking lady would like living
in the studio in Paris, where great pictures were always
going on accompanied by a strong smell of paint and
turpentine.

CHAPTER III.

AUNT GEORGIE stayed for a week at Ververney, and before many days were over
Christine felt as though she had known her
all her life, for, instead of the forbidding fairy godmother which she had at first appeared, she was a veritable good fairy who knew the very shortest and easiest
road into little girls' hearts.

Christine soon talked to her quite as though she
was her own age, and confessed how her career bothered
her, and many other of her childish worries. In the
morning they would sit in the shady garden, and while
Christine would be busy with the beautiful embroidery that the Carmelite nuns had taught her to do, her
aunt would tell her all about America—about the boys
and girls there, and the good times they had, until the
little girl began to long to see her native land and wished

3   25

that just for a few weeks she could run across to see what America was really like.

Christine had never had many friends of her own age, and she had never been happier than during these quiet mornings, or when in the afternoon they would take long walks to gather flowers and see the beautiful views from the vine-clad hills. Their only point of disagreement was in their different estimates of Cherie —the donkey's character. Christine loved her pet so dearly that she could not help being disappointed at the bad impression he was apt to make upon strangers unaccustomed to his foibles. He had always to be started the wrong way, and it hurt Aunt Georgie's sense of reason to start off with your back to the place you were going to. Then, too, he refused to go without an amount of cheerful whipping and urging, which he considered companionable. In fact, he absorbed the entire conversation, so after one or two excursions Cherie was given up as a means of locomotion during her stay, though he was offered to take her to the train when she left, in the knowledge that the knowing beast could never be got to go the full way to the town and would certainly bring her back.

But Christine had another great source of amusement besides the donkey, and that was a rowboat on the
Lefte, a quiet little stream which was bordered by willow trees and flowed gently down to the Seine, having
done its duty as a little stream should by being shady
and cool and turning the little mill up at Petit Ververney.

Aunt Georgie had many happy hours on the river
with her niece. Christine would tell her who all the
holdings belonged to and all that she knew of the families. One fine afternoon they got Pierre, the gardener's
big boy, to row them down the Seine through the swift,
strong current, to the bridge at Ververney. There they
got out at the winding stairway with its worn stone
steps which have been the passageway for generations
for those going up from the river to the town. There
was quite a crowd of boats collected there, for it was
market day, and the women had come in from all the
country round with eggs and poultry, vegetables and
fruit. What a scene was the market as they passed
under the hoary gateway where the tocsin used to be
rung in the days when broils were rife between the
burghers and the Norman lords!

All was peace now, the sun shining down on the great courtyard which was set around with great tables and trestles covered with every kind of fruit and produce.

Geese and chickens in crates, lambs and soft-nosed calves, were exhibited by their owners, who extolled their merits in high Norman *patois*. A babble of tongues screaming sous and francs mingled with the noises of the animals and the twittering of the birds from the fancier's stall. It seemed like some chapter out of the Middle Ages, and Aunt Georgie and Christine lingered for a long time buying small souvenirs, which Bon femme, who followed them, stowed away in the all-embracing pannier.

Aunt Georgie was much amused with the shelves of pottery which were decorated with the strangest figures of Breton men and women dressed in quaint old costumes of long ago, for what was good enough for their fathers is good enough for themselves, these simple people think, and they do not change the pattern of their china once in a hundred years.

The party were laden with a good supply of this old china, which Aunt Georgie proposed taking home with her to Boston, and the huge bouquets they had bought at the flower stalls, which no French market, however small, is without.

It was cool and pleasant going home on the beautiful river, but, despite her happy afternoon, Christine could not help remembering that this was the last day of her aunt's stay, and she knew she would miss her sorely. Indeed, when the parting finally came she threw her arms around her aunt's neck, kissing her again and again, and could only be consoled for her departure by Mr. Averil's promising that before Aunt Georgie returned home Christine should see her again.

The garden seemed very quiet and lonesome when she had seen her aunt drive away, and I think she would probably have gone off to her room for a little cry had not her thoughts been diverted from the parting by hearing Bon femme calling,

"Mademoiselle! Mademoiselle!"

The old woman was standing in the immaculate kitchen holding in one hand a pretty muslin gown which Christine had quite outgrown.

"Bon femme," said Christine, " you can not ask me

to put on that dress. You simply could not squeeze me into it however you tried."

"Surely," answered the old woman, "but with the first communion to-morrow I wondered if some one else might not have need of it. I did not like to speak of it while you were so engaged with madame, your aunt, but if there is nothing else you wish to do, why should you not go up to the inn and inquire of madame if Bettine, the daughter of the gardener Pierre, has a white dress for the communion on the morrow; or perhaps Celeste—' la petit blanchiesseuse '—may not have one. But madame will know; for is not the beautiful muslin of yours far too small, and monsieur has kindly said that it could be given to some one."

All this was said in the most offhand way, as though the old woman had not out of the kindness of her heart devised this errand so that her nurseling should not feel the sadness of the separation.

Christine was delighted to go and see madame and to give any one who might need it her muslin dress. She at once acquiesced in Bon femme's scheme.

"I'll go at once," she said.

"The bundle will be small, and with madame's advice you may present it yourself," went on the wily old woman, who thus saw a means of keeping the girl busy the entire afternoon.

Christine, nothing loath, rolled the dress up under her arm and was speeding out of the garden gate when she was aware of Bon femme panting after her.

" Mademoiselle," reaching her a large straw hat, " forget not your hat; the freckles upon your nose are becoming terrific. The good baby! " as Christine tied the hat under her chin. " Now run along on your errand of mercy."

Madame at the inn was a stout lady who had known and petted Christine ever since she was a baby.

" Oh, it is the dear infant," she cried with as much enthusiasm as though she was not in the habit of seeing Christine several times a week all summer. " Enter," she said hospitably; " we have been gathering most delicious plums; refresh yourself, mademoiselle, after your long walk."

Christine refreshed herself with a big plate of the plums, and indeed she was glad of the cool shade of the courtyard after her hot walk up the hill. After drinking a glass of cold *eau sucre* she was allowed to state her errand.

Madame shook out the white dress with enthusiasm.

"Such a very magnificent gift on the part of mademoiselle!" she said in her French hyperbole. "Would it best fit Pierre's Bettine, or Celeste, or——" Indeed, it seemed as though the entire village would have to take turns in wearing Christine's cast-off dress.

"I would rather give it to Celeste than any one else, madame, because she works so hard and is so good to Cherie; only she may have a white dress and feel hurt at my offering my old one. I do not know if she needs it, do you?"

Madame was not sure. Celeste had great pride and rarely let her wants be known, lest she should impose upon the neighbours, who had already shown themselves so ready to help her in her affliction.

Finally the matter was decided, inasmuch as Pierre's Bettine came in with the joyful tidings that her godfather had sent her down from Paris a veritable confection of a robe. Bettine was Celeste's next-door neighbour, and she was able to report that the little *blanchisseuse* was still without a gown.

" And I never knew it until this morning, when I found her fixing up her black gown for the morrow," said Bettine. " She said that every one had been so kind that she could not let any more wants be known for fear people would think she was begging. All summer she had saved for her first communion toilet; she had white shoes and stockings and the long veil— but then, alas! during her mother's illness all her spare money had to go for doctor's bills and medicine. It would be such kindness of mademoiselle to give her the dress. Although she was fifteen she was ever so much smaller; surely it would fit. Poor Celeste was in such great sorrow not to be robed in white as the others were, she would be overjoyed at such a present."

Christine started up at once to carry the dress to Celeste. As she went past the meadows by the river a bevy of girls, their white caps gleaming in the sun, were busy raking hay, and as they worked they sang over and over again an old Normandy round while they kept time with their rakes. Christine joined in with her shrill young voice and stopped to make sure that Celeste was not among them.

" Where is Celeste?" she called.

"At home ironing."

So she went on to Celeste's cottage, which on the outside, with its high wall and iron gate, seemed in nowise different from the house where she lived herself. The garden, too, was neat and trim, with rows of poppies up the walk, and beds of lettuce and onions. The door was wide open and at the window the old grandmother was knitting. Christine stepped into the cool room, which was flagged with bricks and ornamented with high beds built against the wall. The old woman was quite deaf, but she clapped her wooden shoes hard on the brick pavement, and at this signal, mopping her face, which was red from the heat of ironing, Celeste came in from the kitchen, looking quainter than ever and nearly the age of her grandmother, such was the businesslike air and gravity of her countenance. She wiped her red hands on the coarse check apron which covered her faded patched petticoats; then she caught sight of the dress on her visitor's arm.

"Mademoiselle wishes her dress laundered," she said with a pang at heart that white dresses were bestowed so unequally that Christine might wear one every day in the week, while she, alas! had not the coarsest, poorest one to wear on the greatest day of her life—her first communion.

"No," said Christine, "it is quite fresh; it has not been worn since you did it up before. I brought it for a little present for you, Celeste, to wear at the first communion."

A perfect howl of joy rang through the room. Celeste's aged and businesslike demeanour had disappeared; she sank on her knees with joy, examining it.

"Ah, mademoiselle," she said, lifting her face with her eyes full of tears, "you are an angel. If you but knew the temptation which I had to burn a great hole in the front breadth of this very gown the last time I ironed it—out of sheer envy!"

Indeed, her happiness passed all bounds when Christine drew from her pocket a roll of sadly crumpled white satin ribbon—for, alas! it must be confessed that our heroine had very careless ways.

"You can press it out, I hope," she said in dismay, putting it into Celeste's hands. "It was nice and fresh when I took it out of the drawer, but I am afraid I must have been sitting on it."

It would come all right Celeste was sure, and she

dampened and pressed it in the twinkling of an eye, bringing it back just as good as new. Then from a high black press she took out the tarlaton veil and the white cotton stockings and satin slippers which had cost her so much toil. They made quite a grand show all laid out on the blue counterpane of one of the high beds. The old grandmother looked on smiling and admiring as the history of the donation was howled at her through an enormous trumpet like a trombone.

"How selfish I have been!" thought Christine. "I have been so wrapped up in Aunt Georgie that I have thought of nothing else, and if Bon femme had not been so thoughtful, poor Celeste might have had to go to communion in her faded black dress, when I could have saved her the mortification just as well as not." Being a kind, conscientious little girl, she was glad that the dress had not been given too late, and she made up her mind not to go home and be unhappy because her aunt was no longer there, but to settle down to her ordinary life, that she might have no further cause to reproach herself with forgetfulness of those about her.

CHAPTER IV.

THE CHATEAU.

WHEN at last Christine tore herself away from Celeste's thanks she went home and had Cherie put into the little cart and started out to exercise the beast. She had no particular errand to do anywhere and no one to go and see, so she said to herself, " We will go to the chateau," and pointed the donkey's nose in the opposite direction, whereupon he turned suddenly around and started on the road she wished him to take.

Christine had never been to the chateau in her life, and she had no real intention of getting there this day. The Chateau Beauvoir stood up on the top of a steep hill and was ever so many miles away—far beyond Cherie's uncertain powers. There it stood, however, like a crown on top of the hill, as tantalizing as the blue grass which the little girl kept seeing far away, but never near.

When Christine had nothing else to do she would start on a voyage of discovery to the chateau. There was a little girl living there she knew, for she had seen her in church the year before at the first communion, on which day all the inhabitants of Ververney, including the Protestants, turn out at the parish church to see the beautiful ceremonial.

This day Cherie had reverted to the angelic temper of his youth; he gambolled and frisked, kicking up clouds of dust, it is true, but getting over the ground at a marvellous rate. Christine became quite elated; perhaps she should get to the chateau after all. Her hopes, however, were arrested by coming to a low barbed-wire paling. Planted around in the meadows and on the fences were a series of terrifying notices which read that any one who trespassed on the property of Monsieur le Comte de Beauvoir would be fined and imprisoned. She was about to turn and flee, when a sweet voice called in English,

"Not run zeway! Arrêt! Arrêt! I with you be in ze seconds!"

This extraordinary summons sounded very funny to Christine, and she began to laugh, at which a girl of her own age came hopping out on one foot from behind a tree, holding a shoe and stocking in her hand.

" Pardon, mademoiselle," she said, waving the shoe; " I wad' in ze stream; my shoe she will no on fast; but I have fear you tink me the gendarmes and run off if I calls." The whole effect of the girl rattling out the most strangely constructed sentences while she steadied herself on one of the threatening placards and put on her shoe was irresistibly comical. Christine could scarcely repress a smile, which, however, the stranger seemed only to interpret in friendliness and good-will. Having wriggled her foot into her shoe, she came forward to the bristling paling and said with frank politeness: " How do do? You are ze English artist's girl I tink. I sees you in church in Ververney."

" I am an American—Christine Averil—and you? "

" Felice de Beauvoir; but I likes you all, ze Engleese, ze Americains. I have an Engleese governess; she talk, talk, talk of ze fine time ze girl have. She say I talk like a natif."

Christine wondered like a native of what. But her new acquaintance was so pretty, with her dark eyes and soft curly hair, and her voice was so sweet, and her de-

sire to cultivate Christine's acquaintance so very evident
that she felt that her English, though it might not be
very correct, sounded rather nice and friendly. She
got out of the donkey cart, and going as near as she
dared to the prickly fence, the girls shook hands over
it. This ceremony over, Christine asked if the castle
was near, for she felt that perhaps the object of her
desire might be reached this very afternoon.

"No," said Felice, forgetting her strange English
and speaking in her own beautiful language, "it is a
long drive through the woods. I've not been very well,
and they sent me down to Jeanneton's, my nurse's cottage, which is not far from here. If you will turn
around and drive down the road a little way you will
see it; you passed it coming up. If you will stop there
Jeanneton will give us some cream and baked apples;
she always expects me in at this time."

"That would be nice," said Christine, "only Cherie
is so frisky I'm afraid I'll get there first."

"Oh, I'll come too," answered Mademoiselle de
Beauvoir, and with the lightness of a cat she climbed
the fence, catching and tearing her garments on the
barbed wire and alighting in a heap in the road. The

damage to her garments did not seem, however, to ruffle her spirits in any way, and shaking off the dust she got into the cart.

" Fragments of me are all over," she said, shrugging her shoulders. " That terrible fence takes pieces out of me whenever I go over it."

For once Cherie behaved like an angel. He turned around as quietly as a lamb, and even made no objection to the stop at Jeanneton's cottage. The old woman bustled out at sight of the girls and brought out some delicious puffy tarts filled with whipped cream. Christine wondered what could have been the matter with her friend as she saw her dispose of tart after tart, and when she politely asked her if she had been very ill, both girls shrieked with laughter, as, taking another tart, Felice said, with a sparkling, mischievous look:

" I'd lost my appetite."

" But you seem to have found it again."

" Whenever I don't feel very well I am always sent down to Jeanneton and I get better right away. I used to be here all the time when I was a baby, and I like to come down here and play. You see I don't have to be under surveillance here."

4

"Surveillance?"

"Yes; oh, you don't know. French girls are never left alone a moment; some one is watching me all the time. Papa has lived a lot in England, and he would like me to have more freedom; but mamma—she is so strict! I get so tired of my governess, and the chateau is so gloomy." The girl sighed as she spoke, and Christine felt that perhaps however fine chateaus might be in books, cottages were better to live in.

Jeanneton's cottage was certainly not gloomy with its glowing garden bathed in sunshine and a flock of many-hued pigeons tumbling and circling through the air. It was so pleasant, in fact, that the afternoon passed very quickly, and the clock striking four suddenly reminded Christine that she must hasten home. Cherie was with much persuasion induced to leave a meal of thistles, and the girls parted, expecting to meet again on the morrow, as Felice was to attend her first communion, and of course Christine and her father would be at church. Cherie was glad to go home, and rattled along in fine style, but it was quite late and the afternoon shadows lay long on the grass before she reached the town. Mr. Averil was just packing up his sketching things as she passed the brook, and he shouldered his paraphernalia and put it in the cart, leading the donkey, who was just beginning to feel that he would like to go to Celeste's stable instead of his own.

Of course Mr. Averil had to hear all about the meeting with Felice, and he looked rather grave at first to think how far Christine had been. "Dear me," he thought to himself, "she is getting to be such a big girl I'm afraid it isn't just the right thing for her to go about the country so much alone with the donkey. I wish she had a mother to guide her."

"Don't go so far again; it worries me, daughter," he said kindly, "and tell me to whom did you give the white dress?"

Christine told him about Celeste's joy at the present. So many important events required a long time to tell, and so effectually drove the sadness of parting from her new-found aunt out of Christine's mind, that it was not until just before bedtime, when she was sitting on her father's knee, that she said:

"We miss auntie, don't we?"

"Would you like to live with Aunt Georgiana always?"

" Oh, wouldn't that be lovely? " cried Christine.

And then her father talked to her very seriously—quite as though she was a grown-up person. He told her how Aunt Georgiana had been many years older than her sister, Christine's mother, and how she had brought her up and loved her very dearly. That she had never been able until now to come across the sea to see her little niece because she had ties and duties which had kept her at home. But that since she had seen Christine, she thought it a pity that a little American girl should grow up in a foreign land among strangers and with foreign ways.

" I have been thinking," went on Mr. Averil, " that it would be a good plan if we went home where you could be with your aunt, who could help you to grow into being such a lovely woman as your mother was."

It seemed a tremendous step to Christine to go away from madame, the big studio in Paris, Bon femme, and the lovely garden. America was full of strangers, and she was so shy of meeting strangers; they always made her wish that her nose wasn't so freckled, or that she had some wonderful talent like the infant Mozart or the children in English story books. To leave Cherie and the river and all the places where she had played so long, and just now when she had met Felice—it seemed too dreadful; but she was used to minding, and she knew if her father said they must go it was for the best. She hid her face on his shoulder and said:

" It is a long way, papa."

" Yes, little daughter, but it won't seem long. That's a brave little daughter," he said, patting her soft hair. " After all, I don't want my little girl to grow up without any country. You will see what a good time the girls have there and grow to be self-reliant and independent. There will be lots of friends and cousins there for you to associate with, and you will like it much better than just knowing the peasants down here, who never can be real friends, or the stiff little girls at the convent, whom you have never cared much for out of school hours."

Christine tried to keep the tears back, but they would come and she began to cry softly, though she could not have told why; but the years with her father in sunny France had been happy ones and she was sorry that they were over.

Mr. Averil comforted her and let her cry it out,

knowing it was the best thing for little girls, and he talked to her gently about her new home until she was quite composed.

"The next thing, papa," she said, with a wan ghost of a smile, "you'll be telling me there are American fairies."

"Well, not exactly fairies, still there are fairy stories. Let me see, there is the legend of 'Sleepy Hollow.' Come, close your eyes and let me see if you can keep awake while I am telling you the story."

As you can fancy, Christine kept quite awake to hear every word of Rip Van Winkle's adventures, and when she was curled up in her little white bed she fell asleep with her brain full of dreams of real American fairies.

CHAPTER V.

HEN Christine awoke the next morning the sunshine was streaming over her bed and she sat up rubbing her eyes with a pleasurable sense that something tremendously important had happened.

" Bon jour! " said Bon femme, coming in with the hot water. " It is veritable saint's weather for the first communion."

Christine jumped out of bed at once. The first communion—the day of the greatest *fête* in Normandy! Many of the girls from the immediate neighbourhood whom she knew were to be confirmed this year, and then she would see Felice again, which was an added interest.

"Bon jour, papa!" she called as she heard her father going downstairs, and she put her rosy face out

47

of a crack in the door to be kissed. "May I take my tub to America with me?"

"Yes, dear, if you wish I will pack you in it and send you by express. But hasten down; we have overslept and the sun is high over the garden."

She drew on her long black stockings and buttoned her frock, singing a little rippling French air about Suzanne and bon jour, and then she jumped downstairs two at a time and out into the fresh dewy garden, looking as fresh as any of the flowers, for the sun was so bright that it would have made any little girl feel like running and singing.

Before they had finished breakfast there came a ring at the garden gate, and there, transfigured, stood Celeste smoothing down the white muslin which fitted her to a marvel. The veil shaded her little red face and her rough, hard-working hands were clad in large white gloves. Christine was speechless with admiration at the beauty of her appearance, and Celeste was equally embarrassed. It finally transpired, however, with many blushes and stammers, that monsieur the curé had sent word that if they would like to do so

they could come down and see the procession of communicants start from his garden.

Christine went upstairs and put on the fresh frock
suited to the occasion. The town was bathed in sunshine and quiet until the old bells in the crumbling
church tower rang out peal upon peal. Then out of
the gray gateway fluttered, like white doves, figures in
white gowns with floating veils. Wagons drove up to
the inn filled with communicants from the outlying
towns and hamlets, and soon the streets were thronged
with girls whose spotless draperies shone in the sun, and
fresh, smiling young faces beaming with pride and happiness.

The curé's garden was a lovely old spot with a
closely clipped lawn and old-fashioned trimmed yew
trees. The girls slipped in the gate timidly by twos
and threes, and mademoiselle, the curé's little old sister,
marshalled them into line, and the acolyte put a lighted
candle into each girl's right hand. Christine thought
she had never seen such a beautiful sight as the procession as it wound out of the gateway. The band played
sacred strains, which echoed and re-echoed over the silent hills. First there came row after row of little chil-

dren clad in white with wreaths of roses on their heads; then the boy communicants with sheepish, downcast faces, holding their candles at uncertain angles; and finally the lines of girls in their white array, holding their candles proudly, with evident pleasure in the admiration their appearance excited. Elaborate silk banners floated in the breeze, the band played gaily, and the procession moved up the hill through the churchyard, with its rough-hewed crosses, into the little Norman church which was so old that the knight crusaders might have knelt there to have their banners blessed before they went to Palestine.

There were four girls—daughters of the neighbouring gentry—who headed the procession, and Christine recognised at once, as the white figures swept down the aisle, her friend Felice leading the procession. Her flowerlike face looked more beautiful than ever framed in the masses of her veil, and Christine thought she had never seen any one look so much like an angel.

The simple ceremony was soon concluded and the white procession again fluttered out the door, the band playing triumphantly. Friends and acquaintances greeted Christine and her father on every side, for the

The first communion.

news that they were going back to America had already
got about, and they found themselves the centre of attraction when the pageant had moved on. Christine
felt very proud of the importance the coming journey .
gave her. She put on a quite superior air, and when a
little English girl asked her how long it took to get to
America, she said:

"A month, I think," not liking to confess that she
did not know.

One of the American ladies smiled and said:

"Only a week, dear, unless you have an accident."

Christine felt quite grieved. A week's journey
wasn't so very long; she had fancied America much
farther away.

The big courtyard of the inn was set with great
tables ornamented with masses of white flowers and
candles, and rows of white-veiled figures stood with
bowed heads while monsieur the curé pronounced a short
grace. Long drives and early rising had sharpened appetites, and in a few minutes the good fare had loosened
all tongues and the courtyard was filled with a clatter
of knives and forks and high French voices.

Christine and her father sat at monsieur the curé's

own table, which was spread in the long, low dining-saloon. Christine was much impressed with the honour of sitting down to dinner with all the high church dignitaries who had worn such magnificently embroidered robes during the ceremony. Next to the curé sat a grave little man with gray hair, and a frail, exquisite-looking lady, whom Christine knew were the Count and Countess de Beauvoir.

Felice's place was next to Christine, and they squeezed each other's hands affectionately under the table, but they did not dare speak in such exalted company until in the general buzz of conversation they felt that no one would pay any attention to them.

" Isn't your veil very heavy?" Christine whispered at last.

Felice smiled, showing rows of little pearly teeth. " Oh, no," said she, shaking back the gauze folds.

" I tried on Celeste's," said Christine, " and I thought it would draw my head over backward it was so heavy."

" Celeste! Have you a playmate, Celeste?"

" Well, not exactly a playmate," said Christine, blushing, for she did not think it was quite the right thing to talk about a washerwoman to a count's daughter. "Celeste, 'la petite blanchisseuse,' you know."

Felice looked up from under her veil to see that her mother was not observing.

"Did you ever wash clothes in the brook?" said this astonishing young lady of the high nobility.

"No," said Christine.

"It is more fun than mud pies," continued the aristocratic child. "When mamma is up in Paris I have a beautiful time. I am kept, oh, so strict when she is here, but afterward what fun I have! Sometimes old Jeanneton lets me help her wash stockings in the brook."

Christine gazed at her with wide-opened eyes.

"Of course I shall not do it any more, now I'm so big and have been to communion. Indeed, I'm going to Paris in the fall to a convent to learn accomplishments. Have you learned any accomplishments?"

Christine had to confess that she had no accomplishments.

"Wait until you're older and have been—what do you call it?—confirmed," said Felice with a superior air.

Just then, dessert being put on, the good curé dismissed the children each with an orange, and, as the courtyard was full of people who paid no attention to them, they passed out into the road.

"Let us go to the brook," said Felice; "we will soon be back, and no one wants to be bothered with us."

The girls walked along under the trees which bordered the stream, chattering of their likes and dislikes much as older people do, when, alas! temptation in a sudden guise assailed Felice, though she had been that very morning to her first communion, and though she was old enough to go to Paris to learn accomplishments, for there in a shady nook was the washing box in which Celeste knelt when she laundered linen. In a moment Felice, regardless of her white gown, was kneeling down in the box paddling her little hands in the current. But alas! suddenly the box slipped out between the stones and poor Felice in all her finery was overturned into the water. It was well that at this moment her governess and a footman, who had forgotten their small mistress, were passing by. The water was shallow and in a few minutes the dripping girl was on land again.

Felice, wrapped in the footman's coat, was carried

to Christine's cottage, which was not far away, where Bon femme stripped off her dripping clothes and poured a decoction of scalding-hot boiled tea down her throat— " a *tisane* marvellous against taking cold! " to use her own expression.

By the time the count and countess arrived from the inn they found their daughter sitting up in an arm-chair in the studio looking as sweet as though she was quite incapable of standing on her head in a brook. She asked their pardon so sweetly and was so penitent that Christine could scarcely believe she could be the same girl who wanted to wash stockings.

Monsieur and madame were sorry to hear of Mr. Averil's departure so soon for America, and they went into raptures over the unfinished sketch which stood on the easel. It was not long, however, before their landau drove up to take them home, and Felice, wrapped up in rugs and wraps to keep her from taking cold, kissed Christine affectionately on each cheek and said effusively:

" We will be friends forever."

Christine was so used to French exaggeration that she did not feel surprised at this intense declaration;

indeed, she thought Felice a very jolly girl, which she certainly was, and she thought it would be nice to write to her all about her new home in America and hear the news of Ververney in return.

In a few days the count's carriage stopped again at the Averils' garden gate and out stepped the governess, who had so neglected her charge the Sunday before, with a note all coroneted and sealed from madame the countess asking that Christine might come over and spend the afternoon with Mademoiselle Felice.

Christine was delighted, you may be sure, to see her friend again, and though when she drove up the park drive she found that the chateau was rather small and did not look nearly as imposing close to as it did from the valley, she thought it must be very fine to live in so old a place. The drawing-room had spindle-legged arm-chairs and sofas set stiffly about it, and was so big that when one spoke it made quite an echo. She was dreadfully afraid of slipping on the shining polished floor, and was thankful when she had reached the wide fireplace with its high carved mantel, where Madame Beauvoir stood beside a little tea table.

Felice, though she kissed Christine warmly on both

cheeks, seemed as much depressed by her ancestral grandeur as her guest, and the two girls sat on the straight uncomfortable chairs drinking weak tea out of dainty Sèvres cups and feeling altogether shy and miserable.

The tea drunk, however, Madame Beauvoir said kindly:

"Now you may go and play like good children."

And the permission being given, they hastened as fast as good manners would permit across the slippery floor.

"Oh," said Felice when the door had closed behind them, "don't you hate being with grown-ups?"

"Not always," answered Christine, thinking of her father and Aunt Georgie.

"What would you like to see?" said Felice on hospitable thoughts intent. "There is the carp pool, and at four o'clock we may go around and feed the fish; then there is the old chapel; it's mostly in ruins and it's the loveliest place to play hide and seek. Or my dolls? I'm sure you'd like to see my dolls."

"Do you still play dolls?"

5

"No, not exactly, you'll see. Oh, mademoiselle "—
to her governess—"may we see the dolls?"

The governess brought out a little carved oak chest,
and in it were a collection of the most marvellous dolls.
Their faces were old and black with age and they were
attired in the most wonderful costumes—trains of brocade and garments of bygone times.

"They belonged to my great-great-grandmother,"
said Felice proudly. "She was married when she was
only fourteen, and she had these dolls to play with;
when she got tired of them they were put away, and
ever so many children have played with them since. I
didn't; I wanted a brand-new doll with a cry. I like
new things; everything here is so old. I like the new
order. Now you—you are brought up English fashion
and that is why I like you."

Christine could quite believe that so many ancestors,
like the career that she ought to have, might be something of a burden. But she thought the old dolls in
their faded brocade most interesting. She looked at
them all, examining their costumes and thinking of the
scenes which they must have seen when they were new,
before the French Revolution.

But Felice, who was nothing of a dreamer, interrupted her thoughts by impetuously sweeping them back into their casket. Then together the girls ran down the polished corridors, which seemed of endless length and number, until they reached the old chapel, where Felice immediately disappeared behind a monument and cried "Seek!" But Christine did not like to play a game in the gloomy ruined place, and mischievous as Felice was, she was too polite to do anything that her guest did not desire. So they wandered out into the garden, to the old carp pool, and when the shadow had crept around a mossy old sun dial which had stood there since the old days when even nobles did not carry watches, the two girls sat down on the grassy edge of the basin and threw crumbs to the greedy fish who were hoary with age, for carp live a very long time.

"See that big fish; what a hideous creature he is and how greedy!"

"Yes, we call him Gargantua; he is very old indeed. Christine, I'm so sorry you are going away to America; it's so nice to have you here to play with. I've got to go to a convent in the fall, and I know that I shall hate it cooped up all day long in a house. Papa does not want me to go at all; he says it is better to be on one's honour than to be watched all the time, but mamma is afraid that I won't have any manners. I hate manners. I like to row and ride and fish with papa."

"Poor little Felice!" said Christine, putting her arm around her friend's neck and kissing her warmly. "I should think it would be awful after being on your honour to have to be watched. I'm glad I'm an American."

And Felice, daughter of a long line of noblemen, raptuously returned her hug and said:

"You must tell me of everything American, and when I'm grown up I shall go to America to see you."

So they talked, and they were sorry enough to part when mademoiselle came hurrying down to the carp pool to say that the carriage was waiting to take Christine home. She said good-bye to Madame in the magnificent salon and drove away, wishing that Felice could abandon her ancestral chateau and go to America too.

Notre Dame.

CHAPTER VI.

GOOD-BYES.

ALL this time the little cottage had been in a great whirl of bustle and packing, for Mr. Averil had made up his mind that as long as the break was to be made it was well to make it quickly and be able to sail from Antwerp in the same steamer on which Aunt Georgiana would return. Workmen came down from Paris and put all the pictures and furniture into big boxes labelled "États Unis, Amérique." They made a perfect little house for the piano and rolled it in, and Christine felt very forlorn in the dismantled rooms.

There were many places to be visited for the last time. She went about saying good-bye to all her familiar playgrounds. Her boat and oars were handed over to Pierre's Bettine, who had always wanted a boat to take her fresh vegetables down to the market at Ververney, instead of having to carry the heavy baskets by the long, hot highroad.

Cherie had often spent comfortable winters in the warm stone shed back of Celeste's cottage in company with her own uncertain-tempered donkey.

French people are very domestic and have extremely tender hearts for dumb creatures, and the "donkey of Mademoiselle Christine" had always had the kindest usage at the family's hands. In the general misfortune that had overtaken the poor family their old donkey had died. When it was broken to Celeste that Cherie could not be taken to America, and equally could not be sold, to perhaps fall into bad hands who might maltreat him, and that Mr. Averil was willing to provide a small sum for his maintenance and care, and if she would promise to treat him as well as heretofore, the donkey should be left in her hands, she almost sobbed for joy.

"He shall be as one of the family," she said. And Christine, taking him back to his stall in his future home, feeding him, with parting, carrots, and affectionately rubbing his soft nose, knew that she might rest assured of her pet's happy future.

The last day Felice came scampering over on a little black pony which she rode at a pace that she considered altogether English, much to the evident annoyance of the stiff footman who rode jerkily after her. The girls went all around the garden together and over the dismantled cottage, and when the groom respectfully but firmly said it was time to go they clung to each other, saying good-bye again and again. Then Felice squeezed into her friend's hand a parting present—a housewife made of bright, sticky red leather embroidered with the Beauvoir crest and glittering with bright needles and bodkins—and mounted her little steed, bending down to give her friend a parting hug.

Christine's last vision of her was as she scampered up the steep hill waving and kissing her hand, with the staid man-servant solemnly pounding on behind. Then madame from the inn and all the artists from the other cottages, and even the peasants who had worked for Mr. Averil or sat for his pictures, came to say good-bye and wish them " bon voyage " in the cheery French fashion.

Christine felt a big lump in her throat when the garden gate closed after her for the last time. She had gone back again and again to embrace good old

Bon femme, whose fear of the sea was too great for her to follow her nursling and who was to stay and take care of the cottage. At last, however—no more time could be spared—one more dear hug and Christine was lifted in the carriage and whirled away to the station.

The big studio in Paris was dismantled and shut up, all the beautiful things in it having been packed and sent on with the furniture from Ververney; so Christine and her father went to a little hotel, for there were yet a few days before the steamer sailed and they had some good-bye visits to pay. Mr. Averil went about seeing all his friends who were in town and leaving cards on others, and Christine would sit in the cab in the street and be so full of her own thoughts concerning the journey before them that the time never seemed long. Then, too, Christine had her own visits to pay to the school in the "rue des petits enfants," to see some little English girls, and to take a message to Bon femme's niece, who kept a small millinery shop.

"Now is there anywhere else you would like to go?" said her father on the last day as they were driving home across the "Pont Neuf," the old, old bridge across the Seine which was christened when it was new.

Christine looked up the river to the island where
Notre Dame stands fronting the city, with its great
square towers.

" Yes," she said hesitatingly, " I would like—but I
think you intend for us to go there—to go and see
mamma's statue in the Luxembourg Garden. And I
want to say good-bye to the big Victory in the Louvre.
You see I've been there so often ever since I can remember that I think it would be rather sudden to stop
going all at once. I suppose I shall be a grown-up young
lady when I see her again, and I should like to be able
to say to her when I come back, ' You can't have forgotten me, for I'm Christine Averil who said good-bye
to you so politely before she went to America.' "

Mr. Averil laughed, but he had the cabman drive
to the Louvre. They walked through the great corridors which are lined with Greek and Roman statues, to
the foot of the staircase where in old days, when the
Louvre was the palace where the French kings lived,
all the nobility and flower and beauty of France went
up and down. But they are all gone now, that courtly
crowd, and the great staircase is indeed a worthy place
for the great Victory—the beautiful statue with out-

spread wings triumphantly standing on the prow of a boat, which was erected to celebrate some great Athenian victory.

Christine stood with her hand in her father's looking up at it for a few minutes; then she turned away and waved her hand good-bye. Then they drove to the Luxembourg Garden, where Christine came to play every day when she was in Paris. They sat down on a bench in a shaded alleyway, and through the green opening in the trees they could see the beautiful bronze statue that Christine's mother had designed when she was only eighteen.

Though they sat there a long time, it was still early in the afternoon, and they walked down the street silently until they came to the gates of the École des Beaux Arts, which is the great school where all the painters and sculptors and architects go. Christine had never been there before, but her father turned in at the gate and led her up to the studio where he had studied many years before. The walls were hung with rough sketches, and high up around the walls were written in chalk the names of the men who had studied there and since grown famous.

Christine looked, and there, sure enough, was "Christopher Averil." She was proud to think of her father's name being there.

"Won't it get rubbed out, papa? it's only a chalk mark," she said.

"That's what all fame is—a chalk mark; most of them get rubbed out in time, dear."

But Christine felt sure that never, never would that special mark be rubbed away.

As they came out into the courtyard again, which is full of beautiful old pillars and arches placed there for the students to see, Christine noticed a sweet gray-haired lady with a big boy of fourteen or fifteen, who looked keenly interested when Mr. Averil stopped to point out to Christine the exquisite beauty of some of the capitals. The boy came and stood near to listen, and when Mr. Averil stopped speaking—

"Did you study here, sir?" he broke in bluntly, looking up at him with a frank pair of gray eyes.

"Yes, my boy."

"Are you an architect?" he went on breathlessly. "I want to come here and study to be an architect when I'm grown up."

"No, I am an artist," said Mr. Averil, raising his hat politely to the little lady who seemed much embarrassed by her son's unconventional conduct.

"You must excuse my son," she said; "he is so interested he forgets that he should not trouble strangers."

And as the pair went out Christine heard her say,

"Teddy, Teddy, what could the gentleman have thought of you?"

Christine wondered who they were, and hoped she should meet them again. She hoped she wasn't going to keep meeting nice people whom she would never see again. But the gates of the Beaux Arts closed on the mother and son, and there seemed but little likelihood of any further acquaintance.

The following day Christine and her father went down to Antwerp, where they were to meet Aunt Georgie and take the steamer for home. Now, Antwerp is a queer old town, and although Christine was used to foreign cities and sights, she was delighted with the quaint people whom she saw passing in the streets. Old women with flapping caps and wooden shoes of such enormous dimensions that they looked as though standing on pedestals, great rough dogs drawing little milk

Medici Fountain, Luxembourg Garden.

carts filled with shining brass and copper cans, girls
with copper pails swung from a yoke over their shoulders—went swinging by. Then in the midst of it all
who should she see but the gray-haired lady with the
big boy whom she had met in the court of the Beaux
Arts.

Almost at the same moment a cab came down the
street scattering the crowd right and left, and in it sat
Aunt Georgie. Then, to Christine's surprise, the cab
stopped suddenly and Aunt Georgie, all smiles and bows,
shook hands with the lady and the boy and, as the cabby
whipped up his horse, called back:

"I'll see you again to-morrow."

CHAPTER VII.

SURELY enough, the first people whom Christine saw when they went on board the steamer the following day were her interesting acquaintances of the Beaux Arts, who proved to be a Mrs. Hubbard and her son Teddy, great friends and near neighbours of Aunt Georgiana in Boston. Christine, though rather in awe of Teddy, for she had never talked to such a big boy before, tried to make friends, but Teddy evidently did not care much for girls and patronized her a good deal. There were no other boys on the ship—in fact, no other young people —so perforce they were thrown upon each other for society. Teddy had been in Switzerland climbing mountains, and the first evening out the children sat against the deck house and he related his hairbreadth escapes on icy gorges and glaciers until Christine felt that he was a perfect hero.

The next day, however, all this was changed; a heavy sea was on, and Christine dressed holding on to the berth. When she went to breakfast there were great gaps in the places at the table. Teddy, the hero of mountain escapades, was not there. Indeed, she found him on deck swathed in rugs lying in a steamer chair —a miserable seasick heap unable to hold up his head.

"Good-morning!" she said, sticking the pillow —which the rolling of the ship had jerked out of place —back under his head.

Teddy groaned. "Oh, is that you?" he said, all his superiority quite gone. "Don't you feel badly?"

"No, indeed," said Christine, sitting down cross-legged beside the sufferer. "I've been about with father a lot and I never mind the sea at all. When we went to Greece——"

"Greece!" cried Teddy, raising an interested pea-green countenance. "Did you see the old buildings with the long names off there? I'm going to be an architect when I'm a man, and I've been told that the old Greeks were the greatest architects."

Christine had been many times with her father to see the Parthenon on the beautiful hill outside Athens.

She was not sorry that a topic had arisen which showed that she was not altogether inferior, although she knew nothing of glaciers, so she talked away about her being in Greece until she looked up, and, lo! her audience had paid her the compliment of falling asleep.

Christine took her embroidery out of her pocket, for little girls are brought up in France never to be idle, and sat quietly sewing in the sun. It was not long before Teddy awoke again.

"Go on," he said; "tell me some more about the Parthenon, or whatever you call it."

"No," said Christine, "I think you'd better have some lemonade; it's good for you when you've been asleep," and she went and got a glass, which Teddy drank gratefully.

"You're an odd little creature," remarked the boy as she settled herself again with her work.

"Am I?" indignantly.

"Yes, you're not a bit like an American girl."

"Why not, I should like to know?"

"Oh, you look different somehow; you don't put on airs like most of them; besides, American girls don't sit about and sew."

"Well," said Christine, "if I've got to be idle to be an American girl I think I'll keep on as I am."

"You needn't get huffy just because I said you were odd. American girls are awfully nice, and so pretty, you know. Not but what"—with a great effort at politeness—"I think you'd be real good-looking if your nose wasn't so freckled and you were not so thin and your hair wasn't red."

"Thank you," said Christine savagely.

"Looks aren't everything," went on the sage from the steamer chair, who was feeling better after the lemonade. "Probably you are clever?"

"I'm not a bit."

"Not clever? Well, never mind, people will like you just as much if you're not. Now I like you ever so much, and I usually can't stand girls—they're such geese."

Christine longed further to discuss why she appeared so different, but just then a huge wave struck the ship and her mentor subsided into a heap again in his chair. Thus the friendship between the boy and girl began.

Teddy ceased to patronize her or think she was odd after two days, during which she fed him with lemonade. He was perfectly insatiable, asking Christine many more questions about Paris than she could possibly answer, and relating in turn all about his school and his mates in Boston. Aunt Georgiana and Mrs. Hubbard, sitting with their work and novels a little distance away, would often look up as peals of laughter reached them from the young people. Mrs. Hubbard, Teddy's mother, was glad of the intimacy. Having no sister and his brothers being several years older, she had been afraid, seeing her son grow so big and strong, that he was growing rather rough and domineering. She felt that being thrown so much with a little girl would prove just the softening influence which he needed. She got to be very fond of the girl herself, and afternoons when Aunt Georgie was lying down Christine would often desert Teddy and sit beside Mrs. Hubbard's chair with her embroidery.

"You're a dear little girl," said Mrs. Hubbard one afternoon, stroking Christine's rough hair, for now that Bon femme was not about to continually remind her of her hat, she often forgot that necessary article. "You remind me very much of your mother at your age."

Christine blushed with pleasure. After the strictures which Teddy had passed upon her nose and her hair and her thinness, to be likened to her beautiful mother was a compliment indeed.

" Did you know mamma? " said Christine.

" Oh, yes, from the time she was a baby, though your aunt was my great friend; we went to school together."

" I was so afraid of Aunt Georgiana when I first saw her," said Christine. " She looked so stiff and tall that when I saw her come into the garden at Ververney I thought she looked like a bad fairy godmother; and now I love her so dearly—better than any one in the world except papa."

" Indeed you well may," said Mrs. Hubbard. Then she told Christine how Aunt Georgie had been many years older than her sister, Christine's mother, and that the two girls being orphans, she had devoted herself like a little mother to her sister's education. " Your aunt was engaged to be married to a young doctor," she went on, " but when her mother died she put off her wedding and devoted herself to her father and little sister, who had so much need of her. Then the war broke out and Dr. Halstead volunteered and was killed—my dear, that was many years before you were born, but your aunt has always remained single and always worn black or lavender since the news came of his death. And though people may think she looks a little stern when they first meet her, her friends think she has the dearest, sweetest face in the world."

Christine, who was a very tender-hearted little girl, began to sob, and Mrs. Hubbard drew her on to her lap and comforted her until Teddy, watching them from his chair, was quite jealous, and, walking unsteadily across to them, put his arms around the back of his mother's chair and nearly hugged her head off, crying:

"Mumsie, every one pets Christine; you musn't go back on me."

In a few days the sea grew calm and every one got their sea legs on. Very few were the vacant chairs in the dining-saloon, and as for Christine and Teddy, their appetites were so good that they could have eaten from morning until night. You may believe there was no more sitting quiet and sewing for the little girl after Teddy was well enough to run about. They were here, there, and everywhere, watching the streak of phosphor-escence that the ship leaves in its wake, exploring the engine-room and the cook's cabin; there was no spot they did not visit. One day the chief officer took them through the steerage, the lower part of the ship where the emigrants, who can only afford to pay a few dollars for their passage, are stowed away in very bare but clean quarters. Most of them were fat Dutch fraus and their husbands, who were going out to settle in the West; but there was one little French girl dressed in shabby black who seemed to be alone. The officer patted her head kindly and said:

"I wish I could speak in French to her; she is in the company's charge to be sent out to Manitoba, and she doesn't know one word of English."

Quick as a flash Christine spoke in French, and the despondent girl raised her dark eyes in gratitude at hearing her native tongue spoken. Christine was touched with her sad plight—a friendless orphan going so many miles alone, and she could not think of anything else all through their visit, though one of the men who was taking over some monkeys he had trained for a circus exhibited his pets for their amusement.

When they were again on deck, where the fresh
air felt delicious after the closely packed steerage,
Christine, with a determination that she but seldom
displayed, seized Teddy by the arm and hastened him
behind one of the boats, which was their favourite place
for devising plans secretly.

"Teddy, I'm going to give a concert," she said.

"A concert!" gasped Teddy.

"Yes, a concert."

"But you can't play, and I can't either. Christine,
you're crazy."

"No, I'm not. Didn't the grown-up people give a
concert last night and make hundreds of dollars? Now
suppose we give one; we're sure to make something, and
then we can give the money to that poor little French
girl. Her mother's dead and she's going out to Manitoba to her grandmother, who may be dead too for all
she knows."

The grown-up people had been very busy with their
concert the night before, and Teddy felt that it would
be great fun to do as they had, though he couldn't in
the least understand how it was to be given, when
neither of them knew how to play or sing.

Just then a large, stout gentleman appeared behind the boat dragging his steamer chair into a sunny spot.

"Don't let me interrupt you, little people," he said in a very melodious voice. "You look as though you were hatching a conspiracy to blow up the ship."

The children were great favourites of this gentleman, who was no other than Jan Van der Veer, the great Dutch tenor, who was going to New York to sing in the opera, as the whole ship knew. Usually they would have sat down beside his chair and talked, but to-day they could only stare at him with wide-open eyes, for there in that deck chair placidly smoking a cigarette they felt was their concert. If only they could wind him up like a music box and make him go!

"He wouldn't sing for the grown-ups," said Teddy.

"But perhaps he would for us, and, Teddy, we might get the performing monkeys too; that would make a beautiful concert."

Mr. Van der Veer suddenly became conscious of the four eager eyes fixed upon him.

"Do you want me to do something for you, my dear?" he said kindly to Christine.

"Oh, monsieur," she broke out, "we want to give

a concert if only you will sing, and we will get the performing monkeys that are down in the steerage too."

Mr. Van der Veer laughed until the tears rolled down his face.

"The performing monkeys and me! Do you want me for the performing bear?"

Christine was afraid he was offended, and tried to apologize as best she could, but the singer only laughed the louder, rolling himself up in his big ulster and emitting terrible roars and grunts like the most infuriated of bears. When, however, he heard the kindly object the children had in mind—although he did not promise to sing—he took their concert in hand and helped them make a programme, arranging with the monkeys' keeper for an exhibition.

So that afternoon, when all the passengers were sitting around, the children gave their concert, with some school recitations, and the trick animals, who went through all their antics bravely. Then when the laughter had subsided and Christine was starting to go around for donations for her little French girl, Mr. Van der Veer went to the piano and sang an aria from

Faust in the beautiful rich voice which had made him world-famous.

You can imagine the enthusiasm, how every one applauded, and what a store of coins was rained into Christine's lap for her *protégée*. But all the furor he had created seemed not to please the kind tenor one bit more than the honest astonishment he saw in the children's faces, for they had no idea any human being could sing so beautifully.

"That's how the bear growls," he said laughingly to them, and Christine did not wonder that he had laughed when she had thought he was in nowise so superior an attraction for their concert as the monkeys.

CHAPTER VIII.

AMERICA.

CHRISTINE got to know the captain and all the officers and passengers on board, and was familiar with every inch of the ship, perching in the rigging and exploring the engine-room and the cook's pantry with Teddy. The days went remarkably fast, and indeed it seemed only yesterday that they had left Antwerp before they were sailing up New York Harbor, Teddy, in a wild state of excitement, pointing out the Statue of Liberty, Brooklyn Bridge, Castle Garden, and all the other objects of interest.

The crowd of people on the dock waiting to welcome their friends as they came down the gang plank; the examination of the luggage; the strange new city, which seemed to be " all alike " ; the novelty of hearing every one speak English—seemed strange and new to the little girl who had always lived in France. Mr. Hubbard had come to meet his wife, and the family were going to the same hotel with Aunt Georgiana and the Averils, so there was no good-bye to say to Teddy.

Now, when Christine was feeling homesick and strange in this new land, her first great trial and the temptation to be selfish and think only of herself came as trials and temptations are apt to do just when one is least able to resist them.

No sooner had they reached the Brevoort House, which is an old-fashioned hotel down in the old part of the city near Washington Square, than a gentleman called to see Mr. Averil and they were closeted for a long time together. When he went away Christine was sent for, and she found her aunt and her father talking with grave faces. Then Aunt Georgiana kissed Christine lovingly and left the room, and Mr. Averil drew his little daughter down on his knee and, as he had often done when she was a tiny child too small to understand, told her about a wonderful big piece of work which had been offered to him. It seemed that there was a great national fair to be held in Chicago, and many beautiful pictures and statues were to be wrought to decorate the buildings there, and the manager had sent to ask Mr. Averil if he would undertake a commission to decorate a big dome in one of the most important of them.

Of course you young people all know that this was the great Columbian Fair, and you probably stood right under Mr. Averil's dome when you went there. But Christine had never heard of it before, and indeed she had but a small idea of where Chicago could be.

"Won't it be splendid, papa? Shall we go right out there to-morrow?" she asked. Then noticing a shade on his face—"Why, what is the matter?"

Mr. Averil had to tell her that his going at all depended upon his having a brave little daughter who would try to help him in his work, because Chicago was a long way off and Jackson Park was all torn up with building and machinery and not a place where he could take her.

Christine uttered a cry of dismay. Never, never could she be left alone in this strange land separated from her dear father, from whom she had never been parted for a day.

"Oh, papa, papa," she sobbed, "how I wish we had never come to America! We were so happy in France and you never had to go away there." She cried so hysterically that her father could only pat her hair softly and try to comfort her.

" It's just as hard, dear, for papa as it is for you; indeed, I shouldn't think of going if I didn't think that you would be happy with Aunt Georgie."

" Aunt Georgie isn't you, papa; but I'm going to be good and not cry any more, only I wish I was bigger."

Mr. Averil sighed.

" Christine," he said, " big people have to be separated and have to do things they don't like just as much as little ones. I never wanted to be separated from your mother for a day, and yet God in his goodness took her away and I have had to live without her these eleven years."

Then Christine put up her face to be kissed and said bravely that papa should go, and he must paint the most beautiful picture and come back as soon as ever he could. She dried her eyes and they sat together in the dark for a long time until, worn out with the excitement of the day, she fell asleep in her father's arms.

When Christine awoke Aunt Georgie was coming

softly into the room, and she put her arms around her niece and said:

"My dear brave little girl!"

She brushed out Christine's hair and bathed her face as though she was ill, and indeed the little girl felt very weak after crying so hard. By the time this was done there came a knock on the door, and in came a waiter carrying a big tray which was laden with toast and oysters and other good things for supper.

"We didn't think you were quite old enough to come down to the hotel late dinner," she said, "so you and Teddy are to picnic up here." And the contents of the tray having been cosily arranged on a small table, Aunt Georgie left the young people to their meal and went off to her own dinner.

There was a certain blankness about Teddy's expression when he had entered the room which Christine could not understand. He had looked that way sometimes on shipboard when he had been up to some great piece of mischief. But Christine knew that he never could be so heartless as to indulge in any pranks when she was in such trouble. As soon as Aunt Georgie was

Comforters.

gone, however, Teddy began feeling with great caution in the pockets of his jacket.

"I hope they're not suffocated," he said sympathetically, and then triumphantly held up by their ears a small rabbit and a minute guinea-pig, who while they were alive, as could be told from the guinea-pig's squeals, had a certain look of having been folded and pressed. "I bought them for you in Jefferson Market," said Teddy proudly. "Don't you like them?"

"Like them!" The tears came into Christine's eyes as the little rabbit hopped across her dress, and cuddling her treasures she gave Teddy a warm hug, which the little crushed guinea-pig resented with further faint squeals.

"You'll get along all right in Boston," said Teddy comfortingly when the animals, temporarily accommodated with a home in the scrap basket, had been fed with some greens which he thoughtfully produced from another pocket. "The time will go just like anything, and your father will be back before you know it. I live only two doors from Aunt Georgie, and I'm there half the time. I'll be just as good as a brother. It's a great misfortune to be a girl, of course, but to be a girl without any brothers is awful."

"Yes," said Christine gloomily, "I suppose it is."

She looked so unhappy that Teddy was afraid she was going to cry, and picking up the rabbit, he deposited it in her lap again. This touching attention, as though little rabbits were sure comforters, made her laugh instead of cry.

"Yes," went on Teddy. "You see for a girl you are not half bad. You're not so pretty or so clever as some, but you're what I call a perfect brick. I wouldn't mind having you for a sister one bit."

"Wouldn't you?"

"Not in the least. Now don't you get spoiled and airy and I'll be a brother to you and see that you have a good time this winter." He stretched out his hand and the two children clasped hands, and with the rabbit and the guinea-pig for witnesses agreed to be brother and sister.

"Now let's have supper," went on Teddy cheerfully. "What have we here? Oysters! Toast! Salad! Oysters for me, toast for you, salad for the beastises." And then, with more forethought than one would have

imagined he possessed, he made her plate look dainty
and nice and arranged her pillows so that she could sit
up comfortably to the table.

" When I'm a young lady," said Christine, beginning to feel like her own self again, " I shall declare
that the first gift you ever gave me was a pig."

" A pig! " said Teddy. " A pig in a poke. Look,
Christine, look! "

Tears and tragedies of separation were forgotten.
The children screamed with laughter at the spectacle
they saw, for the little guinea-pig, finding itself un-
heeded in the recent conversation, had become interested in Aunt Georgie's bonnet, which was ornamented
with white daisies, and becoming entangled in the lining, the bonnet seemed to be rolling around on the
floor uttering piercing squeals.

Aunt Georgie, coming back to see if they had been
liberally provided with supper, rejoiced to hear their
ringing voices as she opened the door, but she could
not exactly understand the strange capers of her travel-
ling bonnet.

" What is it? What is it? " she cried in dismay.

At last Teddy's mirth subsided sufficiently for him

7

to extricate the guinea-pig from the mass of silk and ribbon, and he shamefacedly presented the crumpled bonnet to Aunt Georgie.

However, when she heard how he had brought the little creatures for Christine in her trouble, she had no word of reproach for the ruffled condition of her property, but straightened it out, remarking "that it had seen its best days long ago."

At which Teddy, who was her godson, threw his arms around her and said to Christine:

"Now you know you can't help but be happy with such a dear auntie."

At first it seemed impossible to keep the little animals over night in the hotel, but Christine's heart was so set upon them that they were finally accommodated in a wooden box with slats nailed across the top, and thus they were carried triumphantly on to Boston.

We will not dwell upon Christine's parting from her father save to say that she was as good and brave as a little girl could be. We will not see her again until her tears are quite dried and she is her sweet sunny self, happy as can be in her new home.

CHAPTER IX.

AUNT GEORGIE'S big house on Mount Vernon Street was very much as her grandfather had built it—large, roomy, and commodious. Her grandfather and her uncles had been sea captains and travellers in the days when ships went all the way around the Horn to India and China, and the house was full of quaint things which they had brought home. There were great potpourri jars set about everywhere, emitting delicious odours, and boxes of sandalwood, and quaint Chinese things which reminded Christine of the things Uncle Alex brought home in the Eight Cousins. There was one blue jar on the stairway which she liked especially; it had a great green dragon straddled across the top, and every time she went up and down she would stroke the queer grinning monster's back.

The night they arrived Aunt Georgie said:

91

"My dear, I am going to let you choose your own room; there are two little bedrooms in the house, and you may have either of them that you prefer."

The first one they went into quite took Christine's breath away, for it was just the ideal girl's bedroom. There was a little brass bed with a dainty lace canopy over it, and there were goatskin rugs on the floor. The furniture was all white too, and the walls were hung with water colours in white frames.

"Oh, I'm sure I shall like this one best," said Christine.

In the back of the house looking over the garden was the other little room. It contained a small four-post bed and some quaint Chippendale furniture, some childish drawings framed in oak, and a bookcase full of worn volumes of poetry and girl's books. Christine stood for a moment on the threshold wondering what little girl had lived there before. Then she looked up into Aunt Georgie's face, and she knew that it had been her mother's.

"Indeed I would much rather have this one," she said. And the next day Aunt Georgie helped her unpack her dresses and put them away neatly in the big

lavender-scented closet that was about as large as the
bedrooms had been in the cottage at Ververney. There
were some pictures too of the little cottage, of the beautiful Victory, and of Bon femme with her dear wrinkled
face and white cap, which had to be hung in their places.
The bookshelves were quite filled up with The Child's
History of England, Paul et Virginie, and the rest of
Christine's polyglot library. When all the things were
arranged to her satisfaction she felt quite at home and
wrote a cheerful if somewhat illegible letter to her
father in her small cramped French hand.

"I am afraid my little girl will be lonely before
school commences," said Aunt Georgie one day; "but
in another week you will have plenty of companionship, for my brother Robert has written me that he
wants me to take charge of your cousins Jack and Dick,
and I have just had a letter from him that the boys
started from San Francisco yesterday."

Christine felt that she was growing rich in relations;
first an aunt and now cousins. Of course she had always known that she had an uncle who was a missionary out in Hawaii. There were pictures of the big
volcano and of Honolulu harbour in the drawing-room,

and queer straw mats which the natives there weave, in the halls, and a wonderful feather mantle made of thousands of yellow feathers that had belonged to some old native king. But all these strange things seemed only a part of the old Indian and Chinese curios, and Christine could not imagine real little girls and boys living there.

It was hard for her, with her vague ideas of geography and of the distance to Chicago, to fancy any one would ever come to Boston from Hawaii. She looked it up on the map and it seemed an impossible journey. She was much interested, however, over the prospect of her cousins' arrival, and confided the news at once to Teddy, who, true to his word, kept up the friendliest relations with her and was always coming in to inquire about the rabbit and the guinea-pig who were domesticated in a pen in the back garden.

Teddy's knowledge of Hawaii was quite as limited as her own. He had seen a picture of the King, however, who was a gentleman of rather a dusky complexion, and he expressed the polite hope that Christine's cousins would not be very black and would know how to speak English.

Aunt Georgie laughed well at the two children and told them that white people were white people all the world over ; that Jack, who was fourteen, was very bright and much farther on with his studies than Teddy himself, but that Dick, who was twelve—and then she paused and said:

"I think I should tell you that little Dick is lame and his spine is not very strong, so he is not able to study or run about quite like other boys. His father has always written, however, that he is so brave and amiable under his afflictions that every one loves him, so you must just take no notice of his infirmity and treat him like any other boy."

"Dear me, Auntie, can't he play games and things? How sad!" said Christine.

"Not much, dear. He can only walk a little way at a time. I am going to have a Shetland pony for him so he can get about. He is very contented, however, with his lot, and they write me that he plays very beautifully on the violin, which is his great source of amusement."

Christine thought a great deal about the little lame cousin, and, remembering how lonely she had been at first in Boston, she made up her mind to do everything in her power to make Dick feel at home.

Aunt Georgie asked Teddy to tea the night the new cousins were expected, thinking that the ice would sooner be broken if there was a boy to talk to. She drove away to the station, and the children pressed their noses against the window trying not to show the excitement they felt.

"I say," said Teddy, after a few minutes silence, "you musn't let them cut a fellow out."

"Cut a fellow out?"

"Yes," awkwardly. "You musn't think more of them than you do of me, for you knew me first."

"Indeed I shan't, Teddy. Didn't you give me the rabbit?"

"Yes, but they might give you a canary bird," said Teddy gloomily, who evidently had no belief whatever in feminine constancy. "Now," he went on, growing very red, "you know my big brother Frank, who is at Harvard, is engaged to be married to a big girl, and he gave her a ring. Suppose I gave you a ring and you promised never, never to go back on me; you'd have to keep it, now wouldn't you?"

"Yes indeed," said Christine. "I shouldn't break a promise, and indeed I shouldn't want to I'm sure."

Teddy took out of his pocket a heavy tarnished ring which had an enamelled pansy set in the front and a motto, "Dieu vous garde," in half-worn-out blue letters around the band.

"I found this in our attic a long time ago," he said, "and mamma said I might have it. I thought you might like it because it's in French. It means 'God bless you!' doesn't it?" for he was not much of a linguist.

Christine tried it on each of her fingers and admired her little brown paw immensely.

"It's lovely, Teddy," she said, "and I promise always to consider you my best friend." And indeed she kept her word.

They had been so absorbed that the time had slipped by quickly and Aunt Georgie was just driving up to the door with, surely enough, two boys in the coupé. But, alas! for the expected black young gentlemen. They were quite fair with yellow hair and soft musical English voices. Jack was nearly as tall as Teddy and very, very stout, for living in warm countries where one can not take much exercise is apt to make even the children corpulent.

Little Dick! How shall I describe his little pathetic face with its bright, birdlike blue eyes and soft mussed-up hair? He was quite exhausted with the long tiresome journey, and yet there was so much of brightness about him in spite of it that both Christine and Teddy loved him at once. He was very little and lame. His back was sorely twisted from a fall which he had had when a baby, and yet as he sat in Aunt Georgie's strange drawing-room thousands of miles away from his mother and father his face wore the look—which it was never without—of high courage and brave cheerfulness.

Teddy, who was never shy with boys of his own age, shook hands with them warmly, and they soon sat down to a nice hot supper which loosened their tongues and made them feel at home together.

"I suppose," said Dick, pausing over his plate of hot soup, "that you thought we would be rather black and would talk broken English."

Christine and Teddy blushed at this and confessed that they had thought so.

"I knew it," he said, going off into peals of laughter.

"Of course we talk 'native,' but we wouldn't think any more of not being English than you would of being French because you lived in France."

"Aren't you Americans?" asked Christine of her eldest cousin, who had scarcely spoken as yet.

"No, we're Hawaiians," he said gruffly, and continued his supper as though he had a more serious occupation than talking.

"What a bundle of foreign little people I have to be sure!" said Aunt Georgie. "Christine travelled a whole week from one direction, and you travelled double that time from another. When you are all grown up I think I shall take a basket and go around in strange lands again to collect some more nice American children."

"You might be able to carry my size in your basket," said Dick gaily, "but I'd advise you not to attempt Jack's"—with a glance at his brother's proportions—"if you have to carry the basket yourself."

Jack joined good naturedly in the laugh that followed, as he always did at everything that Dick said, but he offered no remarks himself and went on silently eating.

Christine noticed that, despite Dick's brightness, the little fellow was scarcely able to touch his supper. As soon as the meal was finished Aunt Georgie took the young travellers off to bed, hoping that after a good night's rest they would be somewhat recovered from the effects of the long journey.

When Aunt Georgie went into Christine's room to kiss her, as she did every night before the little girl went to sleep, Christine held up her funny enamelled ring and told her how Teddy had given it to her.

"I don't approve of my little girl's having jewellery," she said. "It seems to me it will be plenty of time when she is seventeen or eighteen for her to have a ring."

Christine sat up in bed in dismay.

"Oh, dear Auntie, may I not wear it? I like it so much. It looks so pretty on my finger that I'm sure I shall remember to keep my hands nicer and not forget to wash them after I have been playing, and not bite my nails." For Christine, as I have said before, was a sadly careless little girl in many ways, and the condition of her hands tried Aunt Georgie sorely.

"Perhaps you would," said Aunt Georgie kindly.

"We will see. After all, it is a very simple ring and is not set with a stone, which I could not allow; only you must never take anything else from Teddy without asking me."

Christine promised and put her arms around her aunt's neck, kissing her again and again.

"Dear," said Aunt Georgie, "I think we must make this a magic ring, which not only will keep your hands clean but will do something for Teddy as well. One day on the steamer I heard him use a very bad expression which I did not like to hear from his lips, or think my little girl might hear. So I think if you are to wear his ring he ought to promise something too—that he will never use any words which are coarse and swearing."

Christine thought so too. She kissed Aunt Georgie good-night warmly and fell asleep with the hand which wore the magic ring tucked under her warm cheek.

CHAPTER X.

IT was several days before little Dick was quite recovered from the effects of the journey, but he won all hearts by his uncomplaining conduct. It was a happy hour when he was able to go out to the stable and inspect the small sturdy brown pony named Whiskers which Aunt Georgie had bought for him to drive in a little low tan-coloured cart. The little beast evidently realized to whom he belonged, for when Dick put out his hand he put his nose confidingly down into it. It was characteristic of the boy that all animals displayed the utmost confidence in him.

Of course Dick had to see Bunny and the guinea-pig, now grown double their original size, and by the time the inspection was over Whiskers had been harnessed and they tried his gait up and down the street in front of the house, with Aunt Georgie looking out of the window.

102

For some days Dick and Christine were thrown a good deal in each other's society—for Jack had begun school right away, he was in the class with Teddy— and they soon got very much at home with each other and had good long drives in the afternoon behind the amiable little pony, whom Christine grew very fond of, though he never quite obliterated the glorified memory of Cherie.

The next week Miss Baldwin's school began, and Dick also commenced his lessons. He used to drive Christine and her books to the door every morning and come for her when school was out. It was always a happy moment for her when she saw her cousin and the funny pony scampering down the street, for, truth to tell, her school hours were far from happy. It was all so different from the school in the Rue des petits enfants, where only the biggest girls were in fractions, and the gentle sisters with their sweet voices were always ready to stop and explain the simple lessons, and took more pride in the girls' embroidery than in any of their other studies. Christine felt that here she was expected to know everything. She had to be put into a very low grade with quite little girls, and even they

seemed to spin through quantities of lessons with such
rapidity that after a morning of marching from one
class-room to another and opening books on all sorts of
topics Christine was quite bewildered. She said nothing
about it at home, hoping that she would soon grow into
American ways, but, alas! she only seemed to get more
and more involved.

" What is the science class? " she asked one day in
despair of the girl next to her as she surveyed this ap-
palling name on her programme.

" About creation and creatures," said the girl sharp-
ly; " don't you know that? "

" And zoology? "

" About animals."

" And Delsarte? "

" How to wriggle gracefully."

It sounded a good deal like " wreathing " and
" writhing " and " fainting in coils," Christine thought.
She sighed in despair. And all these lessons coming
on that day, she became so discouraged at her ignorance
that when school was over she rushed away without waiting for little Dick. She burst into the house and rushed
to Aunt Georgie weeping as though her heart would

break. At first her aunt could not understand about it at all, for Miss Baldwin's was considered a very fine school; but when she came to look over the school-books and see so many subjects, she was much surprised, for little girls did not study such difficult topics in her young days.

She kept Christine at home for a few days, and was really distressed to know what to do with the child until she thought of a young friend of hers, Miss Howe, who was educating her nieces Lily and Isabel Norton, and who would not be averse to having another little girl join them in their studies.

So Christine was sent to Miss Howe, and her lessons became a joy and a pleasure to her, for indeed she was not a dull child at all. She came to love her teacher and her little mates, though they were none of them so brilliant as to be studying " ologies " before they were in their teens, but were quite far enough along for their years. There were no more piles of heavy books to be carried home and no more bursts of hysterical weeping, and Christine's school hours were as they should be— among her happiest hours.

There was a great square hall at the top of the house

8

which boasted an old haircloth sofa, some battered easy-chairs, and a piano which was not so new that the children's playing could spoil it, nor so old that it had lost its tone. Here the children kept their multifarious traps, workboxes, games, etc., and on rainy days it was the gathering place for Teddy and the Norton girls as well. Dick had a special place on the sofa, and never mind how his back ached, or how much the rain had given him pains in his bones, he was always found cheerfully lying there in a little heap, his bright eyes and mussed-up hair giving him the appearance of a downy chicken in a nest of cushions. He was always ready to join in anything as an audience, dear little Dick.

One rainy afternoon when the children were all assembled the girls sat in a ring around the fire, with a mysterious collection of lace and ribbons which they were fashioning into a set of toilet cases for Miss Howe. Teddy was as usual doing nothing, and Jack, who neither cared to talk to girls nor seemed to hit it off with Teddy, sat in his corner, for he had a chalk mark on the floor to mark off his own especial place, and got very angry if any one stepped inside of it or touched his things.

Jack always seemed to despise the other children. He never would join in their romps, which he said were babyish. He did not seem able to adjust himself as Dick did to the new conditions of his life. Clever as he was at his lessons, he could not get along with the other boys at school, who called him " Fatty " and scorned his overbearing ways. He had been used to being considered a superior being by the native boys at home, and his vanity had been so fostered and the indolent lazy side of his nature so developed by the easy tropical life, where there was always a servant at every hand, that rubbing against a number of young people who were just as good as he, kept his temper in a constant state of friction. He knew that his father had sent him on with Dick, who was being treated by a great Boston doctor, just to break up his domineering ways, which had long been a source of great grievance to his parents, and that they thought a few years with other boys of his own class would rub off his angles and peculiarities. But as yet Jack had simply retired into his shell, hating Boston and eastern ways, disliking the regular habits upon which Aunt Georgie insisted, and, while not making himself actively disagreeable, showing by his manner that he wasn't going to be soft-soaped into being pleasant and agreeable when he did not feel so.

Christine loved little Dick, and indeed who could help it? She would sit beside him during the hours that he had to lie still, and he would tell her all about his home, of their great tropical garden full of bushes of jasmine and pomegranate, of the great blue bay where he watched the other children dive and swim half the day, and of the volcano which belched forth lava and smoke when it was angry. He knew many stories also that his native nurse had told him afternoons when he lay in his hammock under the fragrant branches—tales of the days when all men and creatures were one great family and the sharks did not bite nor the insects sting because they were men's brothers.

All this was most beautiful, Christine thought, and she felt it must be lovely to live on an island which glowed with flowers and sunshine all the year round. But with her elder cousin she could make no head-way at all. Her advances toward friendship had been treated will chilling reserve, and Jack said one day that girls were not thought much of in Hawaii, especially if they had red hair, which incensed her deeply.

Such was the state of affairs there this rainy afternoon when every one was kept in the house. Jack had ensconced himself in his chalked-off corner, which, along with his tool chest and other possessions, contained a little row of bottles of harmless acids and chemicals which had been used in his chemistry class. The study was one which the boy took a special interest in, and although he knew that there was no danger in any of the fluids, he had warned the girls not to touch any of them for fear of being blown up. He tried to study out some experiments that he had heard the larger boys talking about, but the buzz of conversation was entirely too disturbing. He wished girls didn't chatter so. And just then Christine teasingly called attention to his glowing face.

" Jack looks like a professor, doesn't he? "

Jack turned red and was going to answer angrily when the rest all broke in,

" Oh, yes, let's call Jack the professor; it just suits him."

" I wish you would leave me alone and keep still,"

said Jack angrily. "You chatter so that a person can't think; I never knew such chatterboxes as girls are."

The girls were properly indignant. It was their recreation time and they had a good right to talk; they felt that Jack with his superior airs should be shown that they weren't to be ordered to keep still. So, instead of being quieter, they only made more noise, singing as loud as they could:

> "Oh, give me a ride, dear, do,"
>   Said the duck to the kangaroo.
> "My life is a bore in this nasty dull pond,
>   And I long to get out in the world beyond.
>   I wish I could hop like you,"
>   Said the duck to the kangaroo.

Every one joined in the chorus, whooping up the "roo—roo—roo," and Teddy pounded out the time on the banister to add to the hubbub.

More rollicking choruses followed, and Jack was at a white heat. Little Dick, the peacemaker, with a desire for quelling the racket, began singing native songs, and Jack, who had one soft spot in his heart—and that was for his little brother—leaned back in his corner, angry, homesick, and wretched, while Dick's sweet soprano voice rang out the pretty birdlike words of the song

that their nurse had sung to them when they were
babies:

> Haa heo kanina pali
> Ke ni hiae la i kana helo
> E uhai ana papa ikaliko
> Pua lehua ahihi O U ka.
> Aloha oe! Aloha oe!
> E ke ona ona noho i ka lipo.

But alas! when little Dick stopped singing after
many, many encores, backs were tired of bending over
sewing and legs needed to be shaken out. A wild game
of blind-man's-buff ensued, and then of puss in the corner. Of course it was impossible for Jack to go on
with his work with boys and girls flying wildly around
the hall calling " Puss! " " Puss! " and Aunt Georgie
had expressly forbidden his shutting himself up in his
room when the others were together. If Aunt Georgie
had been at home he would have gone to her, and she
would certainly have seen that his temper was sorely
tried and have kept him with her; but she was out for
the afternoon, and Jack remained in his corner nursing his rage.

When the game was over and the girls had gone
down stairs to arrange their dishevelled hair and Teddy

had carried little Dick off to give him a tune on his fiddle, Jack sat brooding sullenly, his heart full of anger and a great temptation knocking at the door; there was nothing to keep it out, so in it went, as temptations always do when the door is standing ajar for them. He had had a bad toothache some days before and Aunt Georgie had given him some soothing drops to rub the gum with. She had a medicine chest in her room which contained such simple remedies as the household might suddenly need. It was usually kept locked, but to-day Jack knew that it was not, for he had just remem- berer to return the bottle of toothache drops before he came up to the play hall and the lid had been partly open, Aunt Georgie evidently having forgotten to close it. Jack had looked at all the bottles curiously, but the one that attracted his attention most was labelled " Chloroform."

Now Jack, with his love of science and chemistry, had heard of this wonderful drug that surgeons use to put people to sleep, and this afternoon the bad, wicked thought came into his mind that he would get the bottle and put Christine's Bunny to sleep just to see how he would behave. No sooner thought than, I am sorry to say, Jack went down to Aunt Georgie's room—she was still away—and having secured the bottle, went to the hutch and caught Bunny, bringing him into the house under his coat.

Bunny did not like the smell of chloroform at all. He wriggled and twisted and finally lay quite still. There was not so much fun in the experiment as Jack had fancied. He wished the rabbit would begin to wake up, but he lay quite stark and stiff as though dead. He began to be afraid that he was dead, and was in great trouble, for he had not meant to hurt the little creature in the least.

Now Christine, though she had teasing ways, was always sorry afterward, and when she found Jack was staying all by himself upstairs her conscience pricked her and she went up to ask him to come down. There she found him with a candle, for it was quite dark now, bending over poor little dead Bunny.

Teddy was astonished a few minutes afterward when he went upstairs to say good-bye, to see her sitting on the floor weeping, rocking herself in perfect agony over the little ball of fur.

"Jack killed Bunny! Jack killed Bunny!" she sobbed.

Teddy felt of the rabbit.

"It's quite dead. Did you do it, Jack?"

"Yes, but I didn't mean to."

He got no further, for Teddy doubled up his fists and Jack went reeling backward. Then something happened which Jack could never have foreseen when he took the chloroform out of the chest; but bad deeds follow quickly on each other. He caught at the table-cloth to save his fall and the candle and the bottle of chloroform were overturned. Chloroform is a terrible explosive. It went off with a terrible report, and Jack was badly burned while poor little Christine was almost scared out of her wits.

Aunt Georgie, who had just come in, heard the noise and dashed upstairs to see what was the matter. It was a sad sight that met her eyes, and she had her hands full quieting Christine, putting Jack to bed, and sending for the doctor. Teddy went home, taking poor little Bunny's body to be buried, and a strange hush and quiet fell over the usually merry house.

CHAPTER XI

ICK and Christine could scarcely eat any supper they were so sad and upset, and they spent a forlorn evening together. Dick started to tune his violin, but Christine said piteously, "Oh, don't play, Dick," so they sat in melancholy silence. At last when the clock struck half past eight Dick hobbled across the room and said:

"You'll go up now—it's most bedtime—and say good-night to Jack, won't you?"

"No, no, Dick."

"Yes you will, dear."

"No, not if a person had gone and hurt something you loved you couldn't forgive them right away. I know you couldn't."

Dick's eyes shone like stars.

"There was a little boy"—he said unsteadily—"a little boy who always would be a little boy because his nurse dropped him when he was a baby, and one day he went out to see her at——"

"Dick, Dick!" cried Christine, putting her arms around his neck. "I know what you are going to say, dear—that he forgave her for it, and if you could forgive such a terrible thing I'm sure I ought to forgive Jack."

She was struck to the heart to think how unforgiving she had felt, and the death of the rabbit was really such a little thing in comparison with her cousin's being maimed for life.

"Oh, Dick, Dick, you're so good!" she said, rumpling up his hair into most grotesque fashion with her hugs.

"No, no, dear, I'm not a bit good; you mustn't say so," he said, putting his hand over her mouth. "You don't know how awful I feel inside sometimes. I talk to Fred, and you can't fancy how I abuse and torment him and what awful rages I get into. Oh, he used to have a terrible time before I got my fiddle; now when I feel myself getting all horrid I play on the violin mostly and it says beautiful, beautiful things to me, but once in a while I have to let out on Fred."

" Fred! " cried Christine in astonishment. " But who is Fred? "

" Oh, Fred! Did I never tell you about him before? Well, he's my imagined friend. Didn't you ever have an imagined friend? "

" No," said Christine.

" I thought of him ever so long ago. Mamma and I, when the other children used to play hide and seek and run-around games, used to play thinking games; then we thought it would be nice to have some one else play with us, so I thought of having a little play friend —Fred."

" I never heard anything so dear."

" When I grew bigger and mamma was so busy with the native school and the other children that she didn't have time to play so much with me, Fred and I got to be great chums. You don't know what a comfort he was to me before I got the fiddle."

It seemed as though the little boy could almost see his friend in his mind's eye.

Despite his assertions, Christine did not believe that he led Fred a very hard life. They went upstairs together with their arms around each other's shoulders lovingly, and at Jack's door the little man gave her a last encouraging hug while Christine knocked timidly.

"Come in, dear," said Aunt Georgie, smiling sweetly at her, glad that she was not going to rest with angry thoughts against her cousin in her heart. "I thought my little girl would be in. Jack is very ill, dear, and I am glad you came. I think he has been listening, hoping you would come, but he did not want me to send for you. He is in great pain, so you must only stay a moment."

How glad Christine was that she had come when she saw how terribly ill her cousin looked! His hands were swathed in great masses of cotton and the colour of his feverish cheeks was heightened by the white pillow and the cold compress bound across his forehead. Christine had never seen any one who was so very ill before, and her heart nearly burst with compassion. Without a word she knelt down beside the bed and put her arms around his shoulders, laying her soft cheek against his.

Poor Jack! All his self-confidence in his knowledge and power melted away in the shock of the accident and the terrible pain from the burns which he had endured with absolute heroism. He had gritted his teeth and not a moan had escaped him, but now Christine's loving touch was more than he could bear, and for a few moments he sobbed, hiding his face against hers. Then —for he could not move his poor maimed hands—the little girl pressed her apron against his hot eyes.

"Dear little Christine!" he said, and then the cousins kissed each other for the first time—a dear loving kiss that meant forgiveness and toleration on both sides.

For days Jack lay very ill, for to add to the burns he had a high fever. The house was so hushed and quiet that the children spoke together in whispers, instead of their former bursts of fun and laughter. Christine and little Dick were not allowed to enter the room, but as soon as they returned from school they would creep upstairs and wait outside Jack's door to catch the nurse or Aunt Georgie coming out and hear the very latest news.

Teddy, too, Jack's absolute foe, forgot his enmity in the common sorrow. His self-reproach for the part he had played in the tragedy was keen. He never let his feelings come uppermost in this sad time, but upheld the others bravely, keeping Christine out of the house as much as possible and interesting her in the selection of the fresh flowers which she sent every day to the sick-room with a loving message. It was a happy day indeed when the doctor pronounced that the fever was going down, and then Jack mended rapidly, though the children when they were admitted to his room could scarcely believe that the gaunt, hollow-eyed form stretched out so languidly was the fat, robust boy of a few weeks before. But the change in Jack's outward appearance was nothing in comparison to the difference that the hours of suffering had wrought in his character. The killing of the rabbit had brought him face to face with the seriousness of the consequences attending his ungoverned temper and had taught him a lesson that he never forgot as long as he lived. He was shy and ashamed of meeting the others at first, but as his convalescence progressed and he found that his sick-room was made the centre for the children's gatherings, and that everything was given up in which he had been included, his shame gave way to a feeling nearer to love and unselfish affection than he had ever known in his life before.

His first going downstairs was made a regular *fête* by the whole household. But before he left the room he made a clean breast to Aunt Georgie of how he had been tempted to get the chloroform out of the medicine chest, and how he had only intended to experiment on Bunny and had had no idea that the drug would kill him.

Aunt Georgie had never spoken to him of the matter, thinking that he had been sufficiently punished. But she was glad that he would speak of it himself.

"When we are doing wrong, things turn out differently from what we intend," she said gravely. "It wasn't very kind and manly to try experiments on a poor little animal who could not tell you whether it was suffering or not, now was it?"

"Are manly and kind the same things?"

"Yes, dear, I think so. The knights of chivalry whom you are so fond of reading about protected weak women and the oppressed. Now that our civilization has settled most of the questions they fought for, it seems to me that nineteenth-century knights not only should be kind and gentle in their thoughts to all with

9

whom they come in contact, but they should be especially tender of all dumb creatures."

Jack, who was very fond of reading about the brave men in the old wars, looked red and ashamed.

"I'll never torment an animal again," he said.

Then Aunt Georgie told him of the great Society for the Prevention of Cruelty to Animals, which looks after the rights and wrongs of creatures, and punishes those who maltreat them; and seeing a new look of resolution and thought on the boy's face, she put her arm lovingly around him and said:

"Dear Jack, you mustn't think about it any more. It is by such mistakes and such lessons that we see our faults and learn to correct them."

Nor indeed was that all his contrition, for Teddy blurting out that he was sorry to have exploded him, Jack answered manfully enough:

"You needn't be sorry. I've lived out there in Hawaii and bossed the native boys on the plantation until I forgot that I couldn't always have my own way. That's why father sent me here. I'm awfully ashamed of myself, but indeed that won't bring the rabbit to life or make you and Christine ever like me again."

"Nonsense!" said Teddy. "I like you ever so much better than I did before, and as for Christine, she has told me every day how patient you've been; she's the last one to bear malice."

So the matter was all forgiven and, save for Jack's scarred hands, passed out of every one's mind. Indeed, the common sorrow had united the once discordant elements in the household, and instead of being barely tolerated, and barely tolerating, Jack had found his place in their hearts and he appreciated it at its full value.

CHAPTER XII.

BUT Aunt Georgie had received a great shock in the accident with the chloroform, and while she had no intentions of putting the young people under surveillance, she decided to keep a little more with them than before, so she proposed to Christine that Lily and Isabel Norton should come over on rainy afternoons, and that the preparations for Christmas that were then being carried on should be done in company. Every one was to sit with their backs to every one else, and some little screens and chairs with draperies having been arranged, the girls settled down in their corners with their workboxes and mysteriously covered packages.

Dick was struggling with some wood carving, Teddy was doing what he fancied was an architectural drawing, and Jack lay nursing his hand and watching them all.

124

"Now wouldn't you like me to read to you?" said Aunt Georgie.

"Yes! Yes!" they all cried.

"What shall I read?"

"The Jungle Book," said Lily.

"The Pathfinder," said Teddy.

"The Old-Fashioned Girl," suggested Christine.

"Afloat in the Forest," added Jack.

"Alice in the Looking Glass," said Isabel.

"Water Babies," said Dick.

"What a library! Every one has told me what they would like, but none of the books would quite suit you all. How would you like a grown-up people's book?"

"A book," said Dick, "that if we were grown up we would all be sure to like?"

"Yes."

"Oh, do read us a grown-up book," they all shouted.

"I'll begin it," said Aunt Georgie, "and if you don't like it you must say so."

Then she began The Lady of the Lake. At the very first lines about the hunt and the wild mountains in Scotland the boys pricked up their ears, and the girls too listened attentively, although the poem did not possess much interest for them until the place where the Lady of the Lake appears in her skiff upon the loch.

"Is every one asleep?" said Aunt Georgie, looking up from the book.

Six pairs of bright eyes were looking fixedly at her and six pairs of hands were reaching for the work that had been laid down in the interest of listening.

"Go on," they shouted.

But Aunt Georgie would not read any more that day. Too much sitting still was not good for boys and girls she thought. She sent down for some sponge cake, and when it had mysteriously disappeared and the children were refreshed she struck up a gay tune on the piano and they played "puss in the corner" to inspiring melodies.

It rained nearly all that week, for there is a great deal of bad weather during the winter in Boston, and Aunt Georgie and The Lady of the Lake were in great demand during the long wet afternoons. Out of it grew a new and amazing idea, but that was owing to little Dick, who was always full of expedients for the amusement of others.

"Do you know," he said one afternoon after the

reading, " I think it would be beautiful to act The
Lady of the Lake. Jack has acted out home and we
think he did splendidly. Let's try it."

The idea took like wildfire. " Let's have the play
for Christmas. Let's surprise Auntie. Who'll be
who?" they all cried at once.

Christine must be the Lady, but who will be Roderick Dhu and James Fitz-James and Malcolm Graeme?
There were really not boys enough to go around, but
it was finally decided that Teddy should be Fitz-James,
Jack be Roderick Dhu, and Dick should be a minstrel
and sing a Scotch song by the camp fire.

" It doesn't seem as though we need have Malcolm
Graeme in it at all," said Isabel, who was great for
ways and means. " He doesn't do much; he only mar-
ries the Lady."

So Malcolm was left out as well as Fitz-James's " gallant gray," for they concluded that their first idea—to
have Whiskers act the part—was impossible, as Aunt
Georgie would never allow him to come into the drawing-room.

Now began arranging of scenes and costumes which
exercised all the ingenuity of which they were capable.

In the first place, an old plaid bed-spread furnished forth the kilts for the " bold highland men." The lake and skiff, however, were terrible questions which quite paralyzed their imaginations, and the play might have been given up had not Frank, Teddy's big brother who went to Harvard, come to their rescue. He suggested a row of rushes at the front of the stage for the bank and a big pasteboard prow of a boat with Christine sitting behind it as though she was rowing.

Indeed, Frank was the most good-natured of big brothers, and he stage managed and property managed the piece into great shape.

But you must not think that all the days were spent indoors over Christmas presents and rehearsals. The weather cleared off cold and the ponds were frozen over and made excellent skating. If there was one sport that Christine was fond of it was skating. The meadows along the Seine at Ververney had often been frozen over, and she and her father would run down from Paris and stay a few days at the cottage while the ice held. Her skates seemed clumsy enough besides the boys' sharp American ones, and they thought she would never be able to manage them, but she only laughed

and struck out as freely on the ice as any of them.
What fun they all had those afternoons flying about in
the cold with glowing pulses and rosy cheeks! Then
when it grew dark little Dick and Whiskers would
appear to drive Christine home. It was a great game
with Teddy and Jack to see how nearly they could beat
the pony. They would dash off their skates and sprint
up the street after the scampering pony, who always
seemed to appreciate the race in which, of course, he
always came in ahead. The merry crew quite woke up
Mount Vernon Street with their ringing laughter and
merry ways. Aunt Georgie, at the window seeing them
come, as she looked into their bright faces would live
over her own youth with her dear sister and think to herself, " No children are happier than mine."

Amid all the new distractions and attractions of
Christine's life she missed her father more than any
one would have supposed, and when Mr. Averil returned early in December she felt as though her cup
of happiness was complete.

Mr. Averil took a studio in one of the big buildings
near Mount Vernon Street and settled down to his painting for the winter, but he decided that it was best **for**

his little girl with her foreign training to live in an American household, and as Aunt Georgie's house was wide enough for many extra members, Christine and her father continued to live there.

At first Christine felt badly at not having her father all to herself as in the bygone days in France, but he pointed out to her that they would never be able to get along without Bon femme, and he promised that when she was eighteen she should keep house for him, only she must learn to keep things in order and how to manage a house so that affairs should go smoothly. This was quite a comfort to Christine and seemed to dispose of the question which was always bothering her as to her having no particular talents. She might have a talent for keeping house.

Shortly after this talk the medley of collars, laces, and ribbons which formed the contents of her top drawer were put in order. With constant labour it remained so for the most part until it grew to be Christine's second nature to keep things tidy. Although eighteen was a long way off, she found that she did not have to wait until then to be a great help and assistance to her father.

Mr. Averil came home from the studio one day quite worried and worn out. He had had a discouraging afternoon, for he was to have begun the portrait of a little boy, and the child had absolutely refused to keep still, wriggling, twisting, and making up faces until it was impossible to paint a stroke.

It was an important commission intended as a Christmas gift for the child's grandmother, and Mr. Averil was in despair.

"Papa," said Christine, "don't you remember how I used to talk to Beppo, the little Italian model who wriggled so? Now why can't I come to the studio and try to keep this little Tommy Higgleston amused?"

It was a forlorn hope, but Mr. Averil concluded that she might try, and when Tommy arrived the next day Christine was there sitting by the window.

Tommy Higgleston was certainly a beautiful little boy to look at. He was five years old and had a little peachy face like a cherub and a mass of lovely yellow curls. Tommy hated curls; hair only an inch long was good enough for him. He hated being told what a beautiful child he was. Having a portrait painted when he was all dressed up and curled was the last added insult to having been kept clean for five whole years. It was in vain that his mother told him that he looked like a Vandyke in his gray velvet suit with its broad lace collar. He didn't know what a Vandyke was, and he didn't care; he only knew that he wanted to tear up his collar and cut his hair off with his dull penknife.

"Tommy will be good to-day," his mother said, drawing him reluctantly into the studio door.

Tommy wasn't so sure about being good. He knew he had deserved the whipping he had received the day before, and he only hoped he wouldn't deserve another to-day. When he saw Christine he knew that she would stare at him and make him naughtier than ever.

But Christine did not stare. She went right on with what she was doing, and Tommy watched her with big round eyes. First she folded a piece of paper in squares, then she drew some lines on it, and cutting away, disclosed a whole row of paper doll horses; then she took a water-colour brush and asked:

"Would you like them brown or black?"

Tommy was fascinated.

"Brown, with a red saddle."

Christine and the water-colour box did great exe-

cution, and horses were not the limit of her capabilities.
Dogs and cats, girls and boys—she could cut them all
out with nimble fingers. She would tell stories about
them too, so that the sitting wore away before Tommy
had time to be naughty.

Then Christine made some tea for Mrs. Higgleston,
and she and Tommy had some of a very light cambric
variety on the model stand.

" Will you be here next time? " said Tommy as he
went away.

" Yes."

" Then I don't mind coming a bit." And the sturdy
little fellow clattered down the stairs without waiting
for his mother, who thanked Christine again and again.

After that the portrait came on famously and
Tommy and Christine got to be great chums.

Teddy would often come over after the sittings to
look at the picture, and then they would bring out the
big books of photographs that Mr. Averil had collected
abroad. As they pored over the pages Teddy would
tell Christine how when he was studying to be an architect in Paris he should go in his vacations to see all
the galleries and the beautiful buildings in Europe.

" Perhaps you and your father will come over and we can all see them together," he added.

They got in the habit of planning long trips together, spending quite a long time in each place and seeing every picture in the books. They seriously quarrelled one day in the beautiful tiled courtyard of the Alhambra at Granada, and made up in Madrid in the gallery among the portraits of the quaint little Infantas and Infants which Velasquez painted.

Mr. Averil would interrupt their wanderings to tell them interesting stories about this artist, who was a great grandee and courtier as well as a painter; of the boy Murillo painting holy pictures for a few dimes in the market place of the town where he afterward became so famous, and the legends and histories about many other celebrated men and places.

Then when it was time for the studio to be closed for the night the books would be reluctantly put aside, and Christine and Teddy would dance home through the cold streets, clinging to Mr. Averil's arm, and come in with their cheeks tingling with the cold and their appetites sharpened for supper.

CHAPTER XIII.

HRISTINE was much surprised at the preparations that went on for Christmas, for they do not make much of a festival of it in France. The loads of holly and mistletoe, the making of wreaths and garlands, the general tone of high festivity that filled the house, was very exciting indeed. Aunt Georgie's closet was filled with parcels—Aunt Georgie being in possession of every one's secrets and advising wisely so that presents were not duplicated.

It was planned that the children should give their play and have their tree on Christmas eve, and that the following night it should be lighted again and rehung with gifts for Aunt Georgie's mission class. The schools were out for a week's vacation, and as Lily and Isabel Norton had been asked to spend it with Christine, the house rang with merriment from morning until night.

135

A great change had come over Jack since his accident. He was so glad not to be greeted as " Fatty " when he returned to school that he took up training and gymnastics in earnest in strong contrast to the inert, sluggish life which he had led before. His eyes grew bright, his carriage erect and manly, and his heavy silent ways gave way to a more boyish unconsciousness.

Of course he did not conquer himself at once. Over and over again he would sink back into his old inertia and find himself starting to tyrannize over some one weaker. But he had good stuff in him at bottom, and he would begin again bravely. The boys at school, always ready to give each other their due, began to vote that Jack Leaming wasn't half bad, and many of the fellows who had treated him to the cold shoulder at first grew quite chummy with the once-despised " Fatty."

As Christmas drew near, the boy puzzled and thought over a suitable gift for Christine. He wanted to make up to her forever and forever for the rabbit's death, she had forgiven him so generously at the time and had stuck so loyally to him since in all his blue and silent moods. Being of somewhat an unexpressive na-

ture, he was afraid she might not understand how much
he appreciated it, and a very glorious gift he thought
was the best way to show his gratitude.

So he saved his pocket money, denying himself
sweets of which he was very fond, and breaking up his
indolent habits by walking and saving car fares. He
asked no one's advice in the matter. He wanted it to
be quite his own idea, and a few days before Christmas he went around with a beaming expression. He
had made up his mind and the present was found.

Aunt Georgie gave both he and Teddy a certain
sum to purchase new skates, which were to be hung on
the tree and not worn until Christmas day. The boys
tore themselves away from the last rehearsal of The
Lady with difficulty and went off to purchase them,
which they thought was half the fun of possession.
Though their choice had been made for weeks and
weeks, they could not resist the delight of looking over
all the shining blades and seeing once more all the
skates in the shop.

At last, however, Teddy said:

"Two pairs of those."

"No, only one pair," said Jack. "I'm going to
10

buy something else. Aunt Georgie told me the money was my very own and that I could spend it as I liked."

" No skates—whew! " said Teddy.

" Now," said Jack as they left the shop, " if you like you can come with me. I've saved all my allowance for a month, and with my skate money I've seven dollars. I'm going to get the most beautiful present for Christine that will just make her forget all about the rabbit."

" Seven dollars! " gasped Teddy.

Jack as a bondholder walked ahead proudly, Teddy following.

" You know," he said, " Christine is so fond of pictures, so I knew if I got her a picture I should just suit her. I've found a pair of real oil paintings that are seven dollars. I knew they were just the thing she would like, but I thought I would like you to see them before I bought them."

Teddy was sure that pictures were the very thing Christine would like, and was properly flattered at his opinion, as a connoisseur, being asked. Beside such a royal gift as real oil paintings his own present of a fluffy St. Bernard puppy sunk into insignificance. He realized Jack's feeling in the matter and felt that to deny one's self new skates and practise small economies for a month was making reparation with a vengeance.

The place where Jack's treasures reposed was a small dingy shop where battered silver teapots and cracked blue china was exposed in the window. He led the way in proudly and pointed to the pictures which were on the counter. Teddy looked from one to the other and his heart sank. Of course he did not know much about oil paintings, but it seemed to him that they were not usually so bright and shiny. He remembered the ones in the galleries abroad were quite dull, but he knew they were very old—perhaps they had started out this way. He was afraid Christine would like old ones better.

The pictures were very large and framed in glittering new frames. In one a bright-red cow was walking down a steep blue stream while a milkmaid was issuing from a cottage so strange in perspective that when she was inside, her head must certainly have had to stick out of the chimney. The companion piece was the same gay milkmaid driving the cow home up the hill, which it seemed to adhere to as a fly does to the ceiling.

"The frames are real gilt," said the shopman enticingly.

This last remark nearly persuaded Jack to the purchase. He was just going to take out his savings when Teddy's big brother Frank, passing by, saw the boys and came into the shop with a friendly

"Hello, youngsters, what's up?"

He looked at the pictures and listened to Jack's explanation and his breathless demands for Frank's opinion of his contemplated purchase. Then he turned to the man. "You ought to be ashamed of yourself," he said sternly, "trying to swindle a little chap like that out of his money— Those are not old paintings at all, Jack, but chromos not worth a dollar. If I hear of your trying such a trick again I'll report you to the police, so you'd better look out," he continued to the cowed shopman as he led the way out into the street.

Poor Jack was absolutely crushed at the downfall of his plan. He looked so dejected that Frank patted him cheerfully on the back and said kindly:

"Come now, don't feel so badly. Seven dollars is a lot of money. I think your idea of a picture is just the thing for Christine, but I'd go to some first-rate pic-

The Victory of the Louvre.

ture shop to get it. If you like, I'll go along and help you choose."

"Oh, please come," replied Jack gratefully. And just then both he and Teddy caught sight of something in a window across the way, and they gave a loud yell and took to their heels, leaving Frank to follow as befitted his more dignified years.

You will remember the Victory in the Louvre that Christine went to say good-bye to. She had a beautiful photograph of it in her room and the boys knew that it was a great treasure, for when they would tease her to tell them about Paris there was nothing that she would speak of so often as the statue in the Luxembourg Garden which her mother had designed, and the Victory that stood at the head of the stairway in the Louvre. And there in this Boston street, in a shop window, was a plaster cast of a woman's figure with wings outspread, standing on the prow of a ship, just as Christine had described it.

The Italian who kept the shop—which was full of casts in plaster from all sorts of beautiful works of art —said, "Oh, yes, that was the Victory." He had just brought it back from Paris.

It was less—ever so much less—than the terrible chromos, and Jack bought it at once. The boys saw it swathed in tissue paper and put in a big basket to be sent home.

Then Frank advised, since there was plenty of money left over, that Jack should have his skates and that the boys should speed off to get them before it was time for the shop to close.

Jack wrung his hand as they separated and said:

" Thank you for helping me out." And then he and Teddy took to their heels, dashing in and out among cars and trucks and carriages in the crowded shopping streets, and getting to their destination in good time to examine the skates all over again before making their purchase.

CHAPTER XIV.

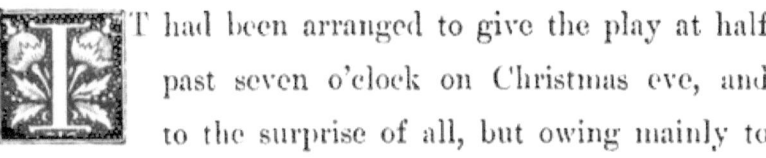IT had been arranged to give the play at half past seven o'clock on Christmas eve, and to the surprise of all, but owing mainly to Frank's wonderful stage management, the curtain was promptly rung up at that hour. The audience, consisting of not only the household but many friends and neighbours, sat in rows in the dining-room just as though they were at a real theatre. There was an extension at the end of the room—a square bay window raised two or three steps—that made a splendid stage, and though the only exit was through a window into the butler's pantry, Terence, the outdoor man, held a short ladder against the sill and assisted the troupe up and down with unfailing patience.

It must be owned that the star and most important performer in the piece was a wonderful moon which

Jack had made by means of glazed paper with a lamp behind it, and the agitating question was not whether every one knew their parts, but whether the moon would work properly or not.

In the course of time you will undoubtedly read The Lady of the Lake and know just what it is about, but the play as they played it, with all the alterations and changes which had to be made because of the limitations of properties and performers, would have greatly surprised and indeed somewhat amused Sir Walter Scott I fancy.

When the audience was well assembled Frank read in a clear distinct voice some verses of the canto, and the curtain rose without a hitch on the stage which was crowded with evergreens. Mr. Averil had outlined a high snow-covered mountain on the blue paper-muslin sky, and the moon soared above it in great style. There were faint cries and windings of a horn in the distance, and then Teddy, in tartan plaid, appeared in evident distress. Then out from among the trees was shoved the prow of the Lady's boat with Christine punting. The moon shone forth with renewed vigour, and Teddy, stepping in among the cat-tails and bulrushes which were tastefully arranged as a bank, got into the skiff and it was pulled out of sight.

This was really a very pretty scene. The dim wood, the horn—Teddy had driven his mother nearly distracted practising on it—and the appearance of the Lady in her fantastically fashioned boat, was deemed a great success.

The next scene was in the Lady's home, the outlaws being collected about a camp fire. Although the logs did not burn, it gained a kind of cheerfulness from a smoking kettle of hot water that hung over it. Several of Teddy's classmates had agreed to be outlaws, and they lounged about, a wild and awful company, while Dick twanged on an old guitar, the nearest approach they could find to a harp.

Then the Lady came in bringing James Fitz-James and asking hospitality for the wanderer, introducing him to her father, Roderick Dhu, and the other outlaws, and while they sat around the fire in amity Dick's sweet voice rang out the ballad:

> Merry it is in the good greenwood,
>   When the mavis and merle are singing,
> When the deer sweeps by, and the hounds are in cry,
>   And the hunter's horn is ringing.

'Tis merry, 'tis merry, in fairyland
  When fairy birds are singing,
When the court doth ride by their monarch's side,
  With bit and bridle ringing.

The audience applauded loudly and demanded encore after encore until the small minstrel felt quite the
hero of the play.

Then the curtain went up again on the place where
Roderick Dhu guides James Fitz-James over the mountains and where, to show the stranger his power, he
whistles, and from behind every heather bush there
starts a canny Scot in ambush. The outlaws, who had
now warmed to their work, came out from behind the
trees with ferocious mien wonderful to see, retreating
again as silent as they came.

According to the story, when James Fitz-James is
on his own land the outlaw challenges him to fight, and
the boys gave a pretty exhibition of their wrestling
powers which was good to see, although it was decreed
beforehand that Teddy must be the winner.

Last came the court scene, with the bandits turned
into loyal and elegant court gentlemen dressed in beautiful silesia cloaks and fur-lined circulars doing duty as
ermine. Lily and Isabel Norton were resplendent in

trained skirts, and waved Aunt Georgie's big feather fans as though they had been princesses all their lives.

Then enters the Lady in her simple plaid and looks about to see which of the magnificent gentlemen is the most magnificent, for of course he will be the king. Suddenly the crowd parts, and all the gorgeous hats sweep off, and all the courtly crowd bow low, and there, with his head covered, in his simple suit of forest green, stood Teddy raising the Lady, who had sunk to her knees with surprise and loyalty,

" For James Fitz-James was Scotland's king."

Every one agreed that it was a very fine play, and the happy troupe tripped down the ladder, glad to get off their trains and finery and assume short frocks and knickerbockers.

I can not begin to tell you of all the beautiful things that were on the Christmas tree; how Jack's heart gave a bound as Christine unwrapped the Victory; or her rapture when Terence handed in a big basket which was full of hay and out of it peeped a soft brown nose, two floppy ears, and a pair of bright eyes. A puppy! A big, soft, fluffy ball of fur tottering on four wobbly legs.

Released from the basket, he stuck out his soft red tongue and whined, and clambered into Christine's lap.

"Is he for me—absolutely for me? Oh, Teddy, how could you ever give him away?"

"Well, I did want awfully to keep him myself. He's a Saint Bernard," said Teddy with pride. "He'll grow to be enormous, and his name is Benjamin, because he was the smallest of the puppies. You can call him Ben for short."

"Or Jam," said Christine. "Why not call him Jam, after the jam that the white queen had yesterday but never to-day?"—for she was just reading Alice for the first time.

So Jam the puppy was called, and he slept at the foot of Christine's bed in his basket until he grew to be so big that he had to be transferred to the rug at the door.

"Everywhere that Christine went her Jam was sure to go," the boys said. And indeed his affection for his mistress grew as rapidly as his legs, which ere long were able to stride up the stairway, which at first he had been unable to accomplish save by hopping from step to step.

But Jam was not the only surprise of the evening.

Every one wondered how all the secret wishes of their hearts had been known; but perhaps little Dick was the happiest of all as he sat hugging his gifts.

Aunt Georgie had a precious violin which had been kept under a glass case. It was so old, the legend went, that it had been made for the greatest master of the sixteenth century, and had been handed down from collection to collection until at last it had been owned by Ole Bull, the great Norwegian violinist.

When he died his wife, who was a great friend of Aunt Georgie, gave it to her in his memory. For years it had reposed in its glass case, but when Aunt Georgie found how highly Dick's teacher thought of his talent and noticed how often his eyes wandered longingly to the old violin, she took it out and gave it to him for his Christmas present.

"Dick must christen the violin to-night," cried the children, who were sitting about the floor amid heaps of wrapping-paper. "Dick, play to us."

So he slipped away to the dark play-room and with his correct ear soon tuned the instrument into harmony. Then he came back and, tucking the violin under his chin, he drew the bow softly and reverently across the strings, which had not been stirred to music since the hand of the Norwegian musician had laid it aside.

What did he play? A Christmas carol? One of the difficult nocturnes that his teacher was so proud of his attaining? No. A Norwegian cradle song that they sing to the babies so far away. Then it changed into sad minor chords—a dirge for the dead; and then to a ripple of joy—joy to be out of the glass case, to be making music—joy that it had entered again into its kingdom of sweet sounds once more.

Dear little Dick! He could not jump and run like other boys, but much had been given to him, for he held the key to a whole world of fancy and dreams, which only the eyes of imagination can see.

By this time it was quite late—time to hang the stockings up in a row in the big dining-room fireplace, for only the larger presents had been put on the tree.

So passed Christine's first Christmas in her own country, and as she fell asleep clasping soft little Jam in her arms—for he awoke and wheezed and whined to be petted—her thoughts went back to all the quiet Christmases in Paris, and she was glad she had had one Christmas like the merry ones she had read of in books.

It seemed indeed as though she had scarcely been asleep at all before the house was astir with little scampering figures in dressing gowns flying to get their stockings.

It was a happy time for Aunt Georgie also, and she awoke to hear their clear young voices, led by little Dick, ringing out the old Christmas carol,

"Peace on earth, good will to all men."

CHAPTER XV.

IT seemed as though so much pleasure could scarcely have been crammed into a week, yet the days flew by and, before they were well aware, holidays were over and school and ordinary tasks had begun again. Christine had not lost sight of the fact that she was to be her father's homemaker and housekeeper. Miss Howe entered into the little girl's ideas, and after her class had well settled down to their lessons she established a little afternoon cooking class. They cooked on a small coal stove, learning to build the fire and keep it at a regular temperature, and Christine was never so happy as when, covered up in a big apron, she was stirring things in bowls or watching things in the oven. Her beaming face over the big dish pan, washing the dishes when the lesson was over, was a happy sight to see, and Lily Norton, ablest of dish-wipers, never could find fault with a single article.

152

Of course the cookery was of varied results, yet,
though Christine never learned to make a loaf of light
bread like Rose in Eight Cousins—for, as she said,
" Why should we make bread when it is so very good
and so very cheap? "—she learned many other useful
things; and since the girls had entire charge of the little
cooking-room, it was like playing in a larger doll house
and gave them a practical basis for managing kitchens
of their own. She learned to market also, for they took
turns in choosing and buying what was to be cooked,
and her only disappointment was that one did not carry
home their purchases in a picturesque basket as Bon
femme did in France, but that they were sent home in
a big wagon.

Tommy Higgleston's portrait had proved such a success that other people brought their children to Mr.
Averil's studio to have their portraits painted. When
they were restless and fidgety, Christine would go over
during the sittings and amuse them, and so she proved
to be a great help to her father. In this way she made
several pleasant acquaintances, and thus she met Marion
Burton, and her friendship with Marion, while it was
never the real tangible affection which bound her to

11

Lily and Isabel, and the boys, was for a time a great influence in her life.

Marion was fourteen—a slight, elegant girl with pretty wavy hair and fine complexion. She was an only child, the idol of her parents, whose every thought was to minister to her comfort and pleasure. She was posing for her portrait playing on a harp, an instrument on which she took lessons, and though she sat exactly in position and never moved an eyelash, in her desire that the picture should be perfect, her face grew so hard and rigid that Mr. Averil felt that unless she could get rid of her self-consciousness he could never get a satisfactory likeness. So Christine was sent for to come and talk with her.

Christine thought when she entered the studio that she had never seen such a beautiful creature as Marion, who sat on the platform in a billowy white muslin with her hands gracefully posed, touching the harp. She felt like a very little girl, although she was only two years younger, and for some minutes her ready wits quite deserted her and she could only gaze shyly at the vision on the platform. But Marion was already rather tired of keeping the pose, and so glad to see some one to talk to that she smiled and made the first advances in the pleasantest manner. She was unquestionably a very bright, charming girl, and soon put Christine at her ease, though, truth to tell, she did most of the talking herself, skimming lightly from one subject to another.

"Did Christine like to go to parties?"

No. She had never been to a party, unless the Christmas-eve gathering could be called a party. Marion had been to a great many parties. Of course she wasn't "out" yet, but she went a good deal to entertainments given by girls of her own age.

"Did Christine like the theatre?"

As Christine had never gone but once—to see Sir Henry Irving at a matinée—she was deeply impressed by a girl who had been "hundreds of times." Marion's beautiful person and a certain quick superficial cleverness gave her a wonderful charm, and it was not odd that she made an impression upon Christine.

She had never seen any one before who was so clever and entertaining, and everything that her new acquaintance said and did seemed absolutely admirable. Almost every girl or boy has a period of hero worshipping, and

Christine's time had come. She thought about Marion a great deal, and counted the days between the sittings when they should meet again.

The afternoons at the studio were absolutely *couleur de rose.* She would always be there first, waiting to catch the sound of Marion's light footstep on the stairs, and would be all smiles to welcome her friend, who would come in looking as gay and pretty as possible in an exquisitely made gown with a hat to match covered with waving plumes. Drawing off her long gloves with the air of a young lady, she would rattle away about the events of the past days, her gowns, her little lunches and dances, the compliments she had had, and how she had been up so late the night before that she had not been to school—all with a woman-of-the-world air which Christine thought perfectly charming.

If Mr. Averil had been listening he would certainly have been surprised and have thought it just as well that his simple little girl heard no more of such gay doings. But he was busy with his work and paid no attention to them.

She had a quick, witty way that seemed superlatively clever to Christine, and indeed it must be con-

fessed that in her admiration for her new friend our
little girl went sadly astray from the sensible path which
her good sense and her education had taught her. She
tried to ape Marion's airs and graces. She wished she
were grown up and went to parties, and took to dream-
ing that she was always a guest of honour at the entertainments to which Marion went. Indeed, if she did not
envy her friend her little enamel watch, her rings, and
all her elaborate trinkets, she certainly grew discontented with her own plain frocks that buttoned down the
back, and longed for stylish gowns and hats such as the
elder girl possessed. In fact, she was in as discontented
a frame of mind as well could be, and would have shown
her feelings quite openly had she not felt that the boys
would make game of her aspirations.

Jack and Teddy were very busy on some examinations at this time, so Christine was thrown on her own re-
sources a good deal, and became more and more absorbed in her new acquaintance. Teddy laughed and
teased her about her enthusiasm until she became quite
indignant, and affairs were not at all bettered when one
afternoon, as she and Teddy were out walking, they
caught sight of Marion sitting in her mother's carriage

outside a house in Chestnut Street. Marion bowed, and Christine was delighted that Teddy should see her friend. But Teddy, though he lifted his hat politely, as soon as they had got by said gruffly:

"Well, I don't think much of her. She looks as though she was saying 'Admire me.'"

Christine felt very angry. She had thought, of course, he would admire Marion, and she had always thought so highly of his opinion that she could not help feeling hurt.

"Don't you get to be like her," went on Teddy— and indeed that was the height of Christine's ambition just then—" or Jack and Dick and I will have nothing to do with you, and "—as a last threat—" I don't believe that Jam," who was puttering along at their feet, " would either."

CHAPTER XVI.

N the whole world there was never a happier creature than little Dick. When his poor back ached and he was forced to lie down for hours he would still smile brightly and be ready to joke with any one who came along, and in his hours of health he was always ready to join in all the fun that was going.

His imaginary friend Fred, whom he had treated so harshly and scolded so often according to his own account, quite faded out of his mind after the possession of the Ole Bull violin, excepting at rare intervals, when he would remark jocosely, "Why, Fred, I haven't had a temper for a long time, have I? But you needn't feel lonely; I shall let out terribly some day."

However, no one else ever heard of these tempers, and if he was depressed and unhappy no one knew, for he would take his violin and play away his sorrow upon

159

it, peopling a world of his own where little boys did not have crooked backs and bad knees.

One day when he was driving along in his little pony cart with Whiskers he passed a great brick building in the front of which was a large glass window almost like a conservatory. The sun streamed down on the glass, and in the cheerful room Dick could see any number of children looking out, watching him, and they were all little children who were ill, or deformed, or crippled in some way, though they did not look at all unhappy sittting there with their toys amid pots of flowering plants. Dick wished that he could go in and talk to them. He had always been a little deformed child among straight children, and his heart warmed to these little ones who were unfortunate like himself.

Just then Dr. McIntyre, who had been trying all winter to straighten Dick's back, came out of the wide door. The boy reined in his pony and called shrilly:

"Doctor! Doctor!"

"Is that you, Dick? Well, I declare!" said the doctor kindly.

"Is that your hospital, doctor?" said little Dick, looking up at the big man with a grave little face.

"It's not exactly mine, Dick, but I come here every day. Do you think you'd like to go in and see the children? Well, hop out, then, my little man. I've half an hour to spare and I'll take you in."

He led the way through the long marble corridor into the great sunny room. It was such a pretty room—with its soft pink walls hung with bright pictures, the rows of little white beds along the walls with little ones sitting up in them playing with books and toys, and the group of children sitting among the flowers in the window—that Dick thought a hospital was a beautiful place.

"Here's our doctor! Our doctor's got back!" they all cried, and those who were able to walk about ran across the polished floor to grasp his hands and coat-tails. A sweet-looking nurse with a soft blue dress and a white cap and apron came in from the next room carrying a baby, and when she found that the doctor's visit was not professional she sat down in a rocking-chair, holding the baby while the doctor took little Dick about.

"This is Mick," he said, "who is always breaking his bones just so we can have the fun of putting him together again. And this is Annie. She's my girl, isn't she?" lifting the little girl, whose foot was in a plaster cast, affectionately in his arms.

When they had been all around the room, the big doctor carrying patient-faced Annie, and Dick had been introduced to all the little sufferers, the doctor said abruptly:

"Now, my little man, haven't I heard you sing? Suppose you give us a song. All these little people like to be sung to."

Dick was never a bit shy of singing before strangers. He wound up the piano stool and sat down.

"What shall it be?" he said.

"Annie Rooney, mister," said Mick, who was no bigger than Dick, although his face looked older.

So Dick sang Annie Rooney and all the street songs and Irish ballads he could think of. The children joined in the choruses, vigorously pounding on the floor with their crutches and keeping time on their trays with their toys to show their appreciation. Dr. McIntyre found that the half hour had slipped away before he knew it and that it was time to be off.

Dick's "Happy Hour."

" We must be going along, little Dick, I'm afraid," he said at last.

" Come again, come again," the children called after them, and Annie, swinging along on her crutches, cried:

" We've had such a happy hour, mister! You sing nicer than the organs."

" It doesn't make you feel sad to see the sick children, does it?" said the doctor as he put the little fellow back in his cart.

" No, indeed; they're just like me. I don't make people sad, do I?"

" Bless your little heart, no; you're a sunbeam," said the doctor kindly.

This was the beginning of Dick's " happy hours." Once or twice a week the pony would rattle up to the door of the hospital and Dick would go in to chat and sing. Sometimes he would bring his fiddle, and it is doubtful if the old Cremona ever had a more attentive audience than those children when Dick gave them Dancing in the Barn and other lively tunes.

He got to be great friends with the nurses and the doctor and many of the children, more especially with the little boy with the old face—Mick the newsboy—who had been injured by falling off a car.

No one knew anything about the " happy hours " for a long time, for Dick was shy of letting his left hand know what his right hand had accomplished. Of course Aunt Georgie knew, because every one told Aunt Georgie everything; but Christine was very much surprised one day as they were driving up Commonwealth Avenue to hear a shout of joy behind them, and there stood Mick, recently dismissed from the hospital, with a great sheaf of the afternoon edition under his arm.

Dick drew up Whiskers and, to Christine's great astonishment, not only bought two papers, but held out his hand and said:

" How do you do, Mick? Mick is a great friend of mine, and I want you to know him, Christine."

Mick grinned, showing an even row of white teeth as Christine held out her little gloved hand.

It was a lovely springlike afternoon when every one was out driving, and just as Christine held out her hand a landau drove by in which sat Marion most beautifully dressed, but she turned her head away when she saw the children talking to the newsboy and went by without bowing, which Christine thought was very queer, for she was sure she had noticed them.

"I'm coming to see you some day, Mick," said Dick. "Whiskers won't stand any longer now, but you know , where I live, and you're welcome to come and see me at any time."

Mick pulled off his fragment of a cap and smiled again. His not very intelligent wits were quite dazed by his meeting the "little singin' gent what ain't no bigger'n me."

Christine, with her sweet face in its aureole of ruddy hair and the way she smiled when she shook hands, remained as a sort of glorified vision in his mind forever.

"They shuck han's with me," he related at home over and over again, "an' they was bowin' right and lef' ter gran' folks in kerriges. You'd thought I wuz ez good ez eny of 'em. Papers! Boots blacked! Ther' ain't nothin' in them lines that the littl' singin' gent couldn't have indef'nit'."

Christine persuaded little Dick to tell her about Mick, and the lame children, and the happy hours. She was so touched that she wanted to hug him right in the middle of the fashionable street, though to have heard

him talk you would have never supposed that he had
done nothing at all, and indeed such was his sweetness
of heart that it never struck him that he had.

It gave Christine's conscience a good prick to think
how nobly he had been using his time while she had
been wasting hers in idle longings to be grown up and
lead a fashionable existence such as Marion found so
enjoyable.

She made many good resolutions to be contented
and happy as she was, and on the homeward drive
did not think once of her absent friend, but was her
own sweet self once more. The boys had finished their
examinations, with great success where they had pre-
dicted failure, and *vice versa*, as is often the case, and
when she reached home she became absorbed in their
triumphs and defeats, and they all spent a happy evening together.

The following day Mr. Averil had a sudden head-
ache and was obliged to return home from the studio
a few minutes before the hour set for Marion's arrival,
and he left Christine there to make his excuses and set
the time for another sitting, promising to send Jack
over for her very soon. In a short time Christine heard

the rustle of Marion's dress, and there was her friend
fresh and smiling, looking like a picture as usual.
Marion expressed her sorrow at Mr. Averil's illness in
the politest manner, and after flitting around the
studio looking at the pretty things for a while, she
said:

"The sleigh is waiting downstairs for me, and as
long as I am not to pose why can't you come and spend
the afternoon at my house?"

Christine longed to go, but she could not do so
without permission, so they finally decided that Marion
should go home with her, and that the call would be
returned as soon as possible.

So the girls got into the pretty sleigh, and the horses,
glad enough to be released from pacing up and down
in the biting cold, whirled them quickly through the
snow-covered streets. Christine could not have felt
grander had she been ushering in an enchanted princess
than when Marion entered her home. She swelled with
pride at her position as hostess, and on the way had
turned over in her mind what she could do for the
amusement of her beautiful guest. Aunt Georgie was
unfortunately out, but she intended getting the boys

into their best neckties and coats and have them come down to the drawing-room to talk to Marion.

But alas for Christine's dignity and importance! No sooner had she entered the hall than it was rudely shattered, for the boys, who were in the upper playroom looked over the banisters, and seeing her familiar hat, boylike, never noticed that she was accompanied, but immediately leaned over to attract her attention, shouting to her to come and join them.

"Come and black up our faces, Christine," cried Teddy.

"How did you manage to tear yourself away from your beloved friend so soon? I was getting ready to go over and get you," called Jack.

And even little Dick, who was usually so tactful, shouted:

"Bring up a needle and thread. Jack's all bursting out of his coat."

Christine blushed for this exhibition of the bad manners of her family. She hurriedly seated Marion in the drawing-room and rushed upstairs. Jack and Teddy, the strangest of figures, careered wildly round, shrieking to her to admire them, and indeed Christine had never seen two such grotesque figures in her life. In place of their usual coats and knickerbockers, they were arrayed in the most forlorn and extraordinary garments. Teddy in a pair of large greenish trousers confined at the waist by a strap, a red sweater, and a battered oil-skin sou'wester, challenging comparison with Jack, who, in addition to white duck trousers, a ragged mackintosh, and a crushed derby far too large for his head, sported a neat pair of small red whiskers and a black patch over one eye. Both boys were so large and well formed for their age that they looked, in the grown-up garments, like a pair of rough young tramps.

Christine's heart sunk within her. Here were no nice young gentlemen to introduce to Marion.

"We're going out to shovel up snow," said Jack in explanation. "The streets are so packed that all the boys from the school are going out this after-noon to help clear them. Teddy and I and the Thatch-ers have dressed up, and I guess the other boys will be wild that they didn't think of it when they see us."

"Ain't we fine?" cried Teddy, jumping around on one leg. "Paint us up a little, Christine. Dick is far

12

too dainty with the charcoal. We want to be real black while we are about it."

What could Christine do in the face of these rollicking boys, who were all excitement and boisterous mirth over carrying out their prank.

"Oh, boys," she pleaded, "won't you take those things off and stay at home this afternoon? Marion has come home with me and I want to introduce you to her."

"I'm glad we're going out, then," said Teddy. "I can't bear that girl, and I wouldn't speak to her anyway, so it's just as well."

"If she wants to see us we'll come right down as we are," cried Jack teasingly. "She will certainly be pleased with our clothes. I'm sure she never saw anything more stylish than the set of Teddy's breeches, and as for my coat," draping the long tattered garment about him, "'tis the latest thing from Paree."

"I'm perfectly ashamed of you, boys," said Christine angrily. "I'm always nice to the boys you bring home, and I think that you need not be so disagreeable about Marion. You scream so loud that she has probably heard every word you have said, and very likely

will never come to see me again because you have been
so rude."

" We'd be glad if she didn't," jeered the boys, and
Christine went downstairs again to her guest angry
enough; nor was the matter made any better by meeting the two grotesque figures on the stairs as she was
taking Marion up to her own room to show her the pictures of Ververney and the place where they had lived
in Paris.

How true it is that pleasures are often much more
enjoyable in the anticipation than in the fulfilment!
Christine would have said that nothing would have made
her happier than to have Marion all to herself for a
whole afternoon. But, truth to tell, the afternoon wore
away dully enough, for as soon as Marion had exhausted
the budget of her latest doings there seemed nothing
else that she was interested in. Christine felt quite
ashamed of exhibiting the picture of the little cottage
when Marion told her of all the fine hotels where she
had stayed when she had been abroad with her mother,
and as for Christine's little stock of dresses which Marion wished to see, she could plainly see in her friend's
face that she considered them a very scanty and un-

fashionable wardrobe. She became more and more discouraged comparing herself to her elegant guest, and when a plate of fresh cakes that the cook sent up had been devoured she was not sorry that Marion suggested, since the sleigh was so late in returning, that they should walk round to her house, which was not many blocks away. So Martha, the maid, put on her hat and jacket to accompany them, and Christine's drooping spirits revived with the cold air and the brisk exercise. But as they neared Marion's house she found that her troubles for the day were not over. A number of men were shovelling snow outside of the door, and she recognised only too well, in the baggy green trousers, the old sou'wester, and the ragged mackintosh, the habiliments in which Jack and Teddy had rigged themselves. The Thatcher boys vied with them in appearance, and they were all shovelling away like day labourers.

Christine hoped she might pass unnoticed, but not at all. The four boys politely took off their very miscellaneous collection of hats as she passed and shouted joyfully:

"Come and help us, Chris. It's lots of fun, you bet."

But Christine walked back sedately with Martha, feeling more than one soft snowball on her back somewhat detract from the dignity of her gait. She thought that boys were perfectly horrid, and knew she never could love them again after the way they had spoiled her afternoon.

CHAPTER XVII.

LEAD US NOT INTO TEMPTATION.

BUT after a good cry, as she lay on her little white bed thinking over all the disappointments of the day, Christine found that her resolves never, never to have anything more to do with the boys, excepting in the most formal politeness, quite melted away. The time dragged heavily, and she was glad enough to see them, when they did arrive, bursting in in boisterous spirits, their garments the wrecks of their original loveliness and their pulses thrilling from the rough exercise.

On their side Jack and Teddy had wisely agreed to stop teasing Christine about Marion and in no way to refer to her lack of interest in their afternoon prank. '

"Just leave Christine alone," remarked Teddy sagely, "and she'll get tired enough of that stuck-up girl. The more we tease her the more set she will be."

So Christine enjoyed a rest from the torrent of

witticisms which usually greeted her after having been
with her friend, and, truth to tell, as time went on,
Teddy's words came to have their just fulfilment, for
before the portrait was completed Marion's capricious
temper and her desire for excitement gave Christine
many a trying hour. Although the latter's loyal little
heart would not confess it, she sometimes took advantage of the little girl's devotion to impose her whims
upon her without restraint. The subtle delicacy of her
face was hard for Mr. Averil to catch exactly, and the
portrait dragged out into many sittings, until Christine
was at her wits' ends to know how to keep her friend
cheerful and amused during the monotonous hours.
Sometimes Marion would be cross and petulant, at other
times most loving and devoted, calling in Mount Vernon
Street to see her dear Christine and making much of her
after having wounded her deeply.

After a very trying afternoon at the studio the day
before, Marion drove up one Saturday morning radiant
and smiling. Aunt Georgie was coming down the steps,
and Marion leaned out of the carriage and asked her
very sweetly if Christine might come to lunch and spend
the afternoon with her. To this Aunt Georgie readily

agreed. Christine would much rather not have gone, but permission having been given, she could not decline without great rudeness, so she hurried on her best frock and hat and went down.

" What a baby you are! " said Marion when they were whirling along. " I don't suppose you would have dared come without asking leave. Now I do just as I like. I go anywhere that I wish to."

This was not exactly true, but Marion was so anxious to show how grown up she was that she did not think what she was saying.

Mrs. Burton was away at a lunch party, but the girls had a delicious little luncheon with Marion's German Fraulein officiating. The beautiful dining-room, in which everything was very new and elegant, did not seem half so nice to Christine as Aunt Georgie's old-fashioned mahogany-furnished room, nor was she so much impressed by the soft-stepping butler who waited as she had expected to be.

" What would you think of going to a matinée? " said Marion after lunch, when the girls were up in her room, which was a perfect little bower of comfort and luxury. She had showed her friend all her beautiful toilet articles, her dainty frocks, and the two or three evening gowns which she had for "going out," and Christine, fresh from the simple cottage at Ververney, was much impressed with all these beautiful things.

"A matinée!" said Christine. "But I'm afraid Auntie wouldn't like me to go."

"Oh, yes, I asked her," Marion replied glibly, and without more pressing, Christine put on her hat and jacket.

She was a little surprised when Marion told the sleepy-looking Fraulein, who was reading a novel in the next room, that they would be gone most of the afternoon.

"Are we going alone, Marion?"

"Yes. You're not afraid, are you?"

"No—o," said Christine, not wishing to appear babyish, but in truth she was not much used to going about alone in the city.

It was one thing to drive around the shady lanes of Ververney and another to pick your way in crowded, winding streets. In Paris she had never gone out un-attended, and with so many people in the family in Boston some one always was going her way.

Marion dodged about among the grown-up people on the crowded down-town streets, with Christine trying hard to keep up with her, and though the theatre lobby was full of people who turned inquiringly to look at the two girls, she bought the tickets with perfect self-possession.

But Christine was not comfortable. She felt as though every one was saying, "What are you little girls doing here by yourselves?" and the sprightly music of the overture could not make her quite happy in her mind. But when the curtain rose, all else was forgotten in the interest of the stage. The play was The Old Homestead—a perfect play for boys and girls, with its fun and jolly choruses. The girls were enraptured.

"Aren't you glad you came?" said Marion when the curtain went down, for, truth to tell, for all her brave outside show, she had been considerably frightened by the crowd, and knew quite well that if her mother had been at home, they never would have been been allowed to come alone.

"Oh, it's beautiful," said Christine, "and—why, there's Teddy!" for sure enough, a few rows in front of them, was his familiar figure sitting beside his brother Frank.

But Marion was very much embarrassed.

" I do hope they won't see us. I wouldn't have them see us for the world."

" But why not?"

" Oh, you're such a baby," said Marion crossly. " You don't really suppose I asked your aunt if you could come, do you? I knew of course she wouldn't let you, so I said nothing about it. Mamma doesn't know of it either; but I hoped no one would see us, so she never would find out about it."

Christine started indignantly from her seat.

" Why, Marion, you told me a lie. You said you asked Aunt Georgie if I might come."

" Well, suppose I did," said Marion, who was really feeling very much ashamed of herself before the blazing indignation of her friend's honest eyes. " Now you're here, can't you sit down and enjoy yourself?"

But Christine refused to sit down. She was going home, and that at once. Then as she looked around she became aware that something unusual was happening.

In the heat of the argument neither of the girls had noticed that people were rising and hastening toward the doors. A smell of smoke came from the stage, and the curtain was hastily rung down. They stood holding each other's hands motionless with terror and dared not stir. The densely-packed crowds of people at the doors seemed to be unable to get out with any rapidity, but Marion would have darted to join them in the despair of doing nothing had not Christine held her firmly by the wrists.

"You must keep still, Marion; you couldn't do anything in such a crowd as that; you mustn't stir from here," she said sternly. The smoke pouring up made her eyes smart, and the tears came into them, though she scarcely realized it.

"Let me go, Christine, let me go," Marion sobbed wildly, and she would probably have wrenched herself away but for the sudden reappearance of Frank and Teddy, who had seemed to vanish most mysteriously. They had climbed into one of the boxes to see if they could find out where the fire was, and Christine called to them with all the strength of her young lungs. Teddy could scarcely believe his senses when he heard

her familiar voice calling his name, but in a moment
he and Frank were beside her. There was no time for
explanations. There the girls were, and the boys accepted the responsibility of taking care of them. Although the smoke seemed dense in the big room, Frank,
who had reconnoitred thoroughly, assured them that if
they only waited until the crowding somewhat dimin-
ished there was absolutely no danger. Still it seemed
a terrible situation—the dark theatre, for all the lights
were now out, volumes of smoke escaping from every
crack and crevice, the hiss of the hose which were being
played on the inflammable scenery, and the cries and
screams of frightened women.

It was probably only a few seconds, but it seemed
like hours to Christine as she stood there, brave out-
wardly but with a fearful feeling at her heart.

"Come now!" said Frank and Teddy at last; and
keeping tight hold of the girls, they rushed them into
the open air through the crowd which was now much
thinned.

And now it must be told that when she saw the
familiar street, the people, the cars, and the snow, just
as it had been when they went in to the theatre hours

before, Christine, who had been such a heroine through the real danger, who had upheld Marion's courage and kept her with the grip of a young lioness from rushing to be crushed in the crowd—our heroine, for such she is, looked at Teddy wonderingly, and then for the first time in her life she found the world swimming before her eyes as though it was no longer real, and she fainted away quite unconscious of all about her.

When Christine came to herself she was lying on the sofa in Aunt Georgie's room, and there was a strong smell of ammonia in the air. She realized that her father and aunt were bending over her with much solicitude, but everything seemed foggy and indistinct.

"Where's Marion?" she said suddenly, trying to raise her head.

"She is all right, dear, lie down; she is safe at home," answered Aunt Georgie gently, giving her a soothing mixture, after which the girl, worn out with the terrible excitement of the afternoon, fell into a deep sleep.

How Christine came to be at the theatre appeared to Mr. Averil and Aunt Georgie as strange and mysterious as it did to the boys. Full of pranks and natural

spirits she had always been, but never in her life wil-
fully disobedient. Marion had gone off into a fit of
hysterics when she saw Christine faint, so that it had
been impossible to get any explanation from her. In
the hours that Mr. Averil sat beside his sleeping daughter he could not help feeling that if his dear, gentle
little Christine had changed in so few months into a
girl who would go to a matinée without permission, he
wished he had never left France, where little girls do
not learn such independent ways.

The next day, though feeling very ill and weak,
Christine was able to sit up in bed and eat the dainty
meals which cook sent up to her. The doctor came and
announced that she was doing finely, and that a rest in
bed for a few days was all she needed to set her up all
right. He cautioned Aunt Georgie not to speak to her
of the fire.

"Let the shock wear off her mind as quickly as possible," he said. And so nothing was said on the subject,
and indeed Christine was glad, for she did not like to
tell the part which Marion had played in the matter.

So the older people waited until the time should
come when she should speak of her own accord. But

there was one person who, in his blunt, honest heart, felt that there could never be any explanation which would make him trust and believe in Christine as he had done before, and that person was Teddy.

He had always disliked girls—fibbing, sneaking things he called them—and Christine had only won his heart by her lack of airs and evident honesty. All her sweet little-womanly ways had twined themselves deeply around his heart, and now to find that she was just the same as all the others was too bad. Righteous indignation filled Teddy's mind, and he asked no questions about her recovery, talking to the boys about general subjects as though there was no little girl lying upstairs whose ruddy head had once been a veritable sunbeam in the house.

Indeed, when the boys were allowed to go up for a few minutes to see her, Teddy would have gladly slipped home, but Aunt Georgie, having no idea of what was passing in his mind, asked him to carry up some flowers, and there was no way of his escaping.

But Christine knew what was the matter the minute she saw him. This stern judicial Teddy was not her dear friend at all; all the brightness died out of her face at his cool greeting, and she turned her face to the wall to keep him from seeing her tears.

During the afternoon Teddy quieted his conscience by saying that it was quite right to be angry with a person for just cause, and that he had been none too cool to Christine. But after he had gone to bed that night he could not sleep for thinking how sweet and expectant she had looked sitting by the fire in her pretty blue wrapper, and how sadly she had turned away.

Teddy got up and looked out the window. There was Aunt Georgie's house and the night light burning in Christine's room. Suppose she should die— how he wished he could see her that moment and tell her she mustn't feel badly! He put on his clothes, though he did not know exactly why, and just then, as the clock was striking eleven, he saw one of the servants, who had been spending the evening out, stop at the area gate. Quick as a flash Teddy was out of the house, and the tired cook, who was used to seeing him in and out at all hours, made no objections to letting him in. He crept upstairs to Christine's door and listened.

"Who is there?" said Christine softly, for, just as

13

Teddy had imagined, she had been lying awake wondering if they would ever be friends again.

" It's Teddy."

Then in a moment Christine, wrapped up in the big
blue gown which made her look very tall and stately,
came out into the hall, and he drew her down on the
stairs beside him. They didn't say one word for some
time, but somehow, sitting there, Christine knew that
everything was quite right again between them.

" I'll tell you all about it, Teddy," she said bravely
at last.

" No, indeed, you needn't; it's not necessary."

" Yes it is." And then, not blaming Marion more
than she could help, Christine told him just how they
had gone to the matinee.

He said no further word of dispraise concerning
the friendship, for he thought it had been tried and
found wanting.

" Dear Chris! " he said, when she had finished,
" here I've been so angry at you when you were not
to blame at all, and you have been a perfect heroine.
You looked as brave as could be when I saw you standing up there in the theatre."

" I was scared enough inside," said Christine, " I can tell you."

" I'm sorry that I was so cross before you told me. I ought to have believed in you anyway. You'd believe in me I know, even if everything was against me," he said contritely.

" Yes, I should," said Christine, and she kept her word. Through all the trials and temptations of Teddy's boyhood and manhood, however much he was misjudged by others, he could always comfort himself with the thought that she understood him and believed no evil.

Then, lest, in spite of the woolly dressing gown, she should take cold, Teddy begged her to go back to bed, and with a warm parting hug of complete reconciliation, Christine ran back to her room and Teddy flew back to his own house, where happily, the street being a quiet one, no one had noticed the front door was ajar.

Teddy went over the next morning and told Aunt Georgie the whole story, and a great load was lifted from her mind. She went straight to Christine's room and held the girl in her arms, kissing her again and again to think how bravely she had acted.

Christine's recovery, now that her mind was at rest, was very rapid, and great was the jubilation among the boys when she was able to come downstairs for the first time.

Lying on the sofa in the playroom holding one of Aunt Georgie's hands and fondling Jam's soft head with the other, the three boys grouped about at her feet and gazing at her with loving eyes, Christine felt that with such dear true friends she had been foolish to long for other companionship. The tears came to her eyes again to think of Marion's conduct, and the boys, seeing her look so woebegone, began to cut up antics and dance about the sofa, singing " Now she's a jolly good fellow " until she was half laughing amid her tears.

Then Teddy and Jack, for her further cheering, stripped off their coats and gave a great exhibition of strength, hanging from the doors, standing on their heads, swinging Indian clubs in all sorts of gyrations, and executing many remarkable antics which they called the circus.

Aunt Georgie sat beside Christine, almost afraid to let her out of her sight, and they laughed until they were quite exhausted at the boys' funny tricks, which wound up in great shape with a hippodrome—a race between Jam and the pussy.

When supper was ready the boys carried Christine downstairs on their clasped hands. It was an extra good one, and it seemed as though no one could do enough to show how thankful they were that she had escaped such terrible peril and was their dear companion once more.

CHAPTER XVIII.

CONTENTMENT IS BETTER THAN WEALTH.

SOON Christine was running about as well and happy as ever, but her mind was not perfectly at ease until one afternoon when her father came home early from his studio and she found him sitting by the fire. She climbed up onto his knee and told him of all her sad impatience during the past weeks; how she had wanted to be fashionable, and to have fine frocks like Marion's, and had disliked her own pretty clothes and even her dear home.

" I even wanted to lace in my waist; it seemed awfully big," she said.

Mr. Averil had no word of reproof to utter. He thought she had worked out the lesson for herself.

" Well, dear, one of these days you will be a young lady, I suppose, but I hope you will have the good sense not to lace in your waist. You must never expect, even though you grow to be quite an old woman, to be anything but a little girl to father," was all he said kindly.

She was glad enough to remain a little girl now, for she had had her first experience of the outside world and it had been a bitter one. She had been taught a hard lesson, and never, never again, though she made many mistakes, was she easily led away by appearances.

The boys vied with each other in making much of her, and it was a proud moment for Dick when he took her to drive for the first time, Whiskers being more than usually spry in dashing in and out among the big carriages. The afternoon was warm and sunny, and many of their acquaintances were out driving. They passed Marion, who smiled and waved her hand, and many other people smiled pleasantly at the funny little equipage with the two children's bright faces beaming out of the fur robes.

There at the crossing stood Mick, and when he saw them coming he grinned from ear to ear.

" Glad to see yer out again, miss," he managed to get out.

" I'm coming to see you very soon, now my cousin's better," said Dick politely. " Good-bye," as the pony, unwilling to stand, took the bit in his teeth and scampered away.

"Don't you think I could go too?" said Christine. "I used to know lots of poor people in Ververney. Every one was poor there, and even when they were quite little they used to have to work instead of playing. There was Celeste—'la petit blanchisseuse.' I gave her my old white dress for her first communion."

But when a visit to Mick's mother was broached to Aunt Georgie she shook her head.

"Poor people in America don't live in nice clean cottages, but in rickety old tenements. I think I had better go with Dick myself and find out if the family stands in any need of assistance," she said. So the next afternoon they started out to hunt up the Rafferty family.

The address which Mick had given was way down in the east end, and Aunt Georgie, who was used to "slumming," was not surprised at the dirty streets, but it brought little Dick's heart up in his mouth to see so many shivering little children thinly clad on such a cold winter's day with the east wind blowing.

In answer to their inquiries for Mick Rafferty the

paper boy, they were told to go upstairs three flights back; and they toiled up the steep black stairway in such a very old rickety building that Aunt Georgie was glad enough that she had accompanied her small nephew.

The Rafferty household was evidently not used to receiving guests, for when, after a shrill "Come in!" Dick pushed open the door, the inhabitants of the room gazed at him open-mouthed. In the centre of the room stood a little girl with one side of her face swollen to enormous dimensions and a great red flannel rag tied around it, the large ends standing up on top of her head like rabbits' ears. In her arms she held a heavy baby who was evidently perfectly entranced with trying to catch hold of the red flannel, which wobbled about grotesquely as she moved her head.

"Mother's out and Mick's out," said this extraordinary little person, recovering from her surprise at seeing such unexpected callers. "You're the little singin' gent what Mick talks about, ain't yer?" she queried as Dick advanced into the room. "Don't yer be feared of ketchin' my face; its toothache, not mumps. Mick 'ill be in soon. Won't yer come in and wait fer him?"

She deposited the baby on the floor and hospitably dusted off two chairs with her apron, and, when her visitors were seated, patiently picked the child up again, standing holding him as she talked.

Aunt Georgie's quick eyes were noting the contents of the room. Bare and poor as it was, it was clean. The baby, though ragged, was evidently not neglected, and the little children were sweet and clean. It was fearfully cold, however; there had evidently been no fire in the stove that day, and the cupboard, of which the door stood open, was quite empty.

"Mother's out looking for work," said Bridget. "Mick will bring in some coals and things when he comes if he's had a good day. The fire's only been out a little while."

"Do you stay and take care of the children?" said Aunt Georgie, smiling at the odd little face peering out of the big red flannel bandage.

"Yes"—the child drew herself up proudly—"I'm a 'Little Mother.' There was a young lady came round last fall and axed me to jine her 'sociation. They teaches us to sew and cook, and we leaves our babies in the nursery next door——"

Just then Mick's face appeared in the doorway, and, oblivious of the presence of the strangers, the babies set up a loud hand-clapping. Mick pulled off his cap and showed his white teeth in an enormous grin. In one hand he was carrying a scuttle of coal, and various parcels peeped out of his pockets.

"Yer must me excusin' there bein' no fire," apologetically. "Mother's out of work and things is kinder run out. I'd a good day and we'll soon be comf'table."

Contentment and happiness beamed on the children's faces as he lit the fire with a few treasured bits of wood.

Aunt Georgie was afraid to stay longer for fear of taking cold, but just then the children cried "Mother! Mother!" and the baby toddled on his uncertain legs toward the door.

Then what a surprise! Who should Mrs. Rafferty be but a maid of Aunt Georgie's who had left her to be married years before. She shed tears of joy to see her old mistress, and when Aunt Georgie told her that she was in need of a laundress and would be glad for her old servant to have the place, no happier sight can be imagined than the gratitude on their faces.

The dingy tenement was much too far away for Mrs. Rafferty to go back and forward to her work, so Aunt Georgie advised her moving to a clean little flat in a model tenement not so far from Mount Vernon Street.

The settling of the family in their new abode was a great amusement to the children, who always called them "Dick's family." The girls did not wish to be left out of the fun, and, under Aunt Georgie's supervision, they basted and got ready for the machine many neat little garments for the children, and necessary bed and house linen.

Aunt Georgie cut and planned and Martha, the maid, sewed on the machine, so that the work was soon completed. This led to the girls wishing to keep up a sewing-circle, and Aunt Georgie read aloud David Copperfield and Our Mutual Friend while they were at work.

At first the boys laughed at the sewing, but they soon got into the habit of coming to hear the reading, for they did not like to drop behind in the interesting history of the Boffins.

"I wish I knew how to sew," said Teddy one day.

" I often wonder what I shall do about my buttons and things when I'm studying in Paris. I don't see why boys are not taught to sew as well as girls. Christine"— for he was a very masterful young man and growing so big that his Paris studies did not seem so very far away—" Christine, teach me to sew? "

He stuck her little gold thimble on his finger, and seizing a big needle, tried to thread it. He tried and tried, but his fingers were so big and the needle so little that it seemed impossible he would ever hit the eye.

Then Jack and Dick, anxious to show their abilities, were set to threading needles. At last Teddy held up triumphantly a very sticky needle with a rather grayish thread through the eye. Amid peals of laughter the lesson proceeded to stitching.

" Whew! " said Teddy, straightening up his big back after a short attempt at a seam. " Does it always make one's back ache so? "

Aunt Georgie stopped reading and examined the pieces which the boys held up proudly. Teddy's had large stitches gathering and puckering the cloth, Dick had forgotten to make a knot and the thread had drawn through, and Jack's line was of a curving and waving nature.

"Practice will improve you all," she said. "Keep on and see if by the time we have finished the book you won't be able to show me a trim seam and secure buttons."

So each sewing day the boys practised with their needles, and though the results would never be called "fine sewing," it was a practical lesson which stood them in good stead.

Christine gave them each a housewife, and though they laughed and put them aside among their boyish possessions, in after-years, when Jack was in college and Teddy away in Paris, their thoughts were often brought back to the little sewing-circle as they sewed on their own buttons and put the needles back in the cases Christine had given them.

But all this is getting way ahead of the Raffertys' moving, which was a great event to our young people. As soon as the most necessary articles were finished they were taken round to the model tenement, at which the family had not yet arrived, and Christine laid all the sheets, towels, and pillow-slips in neat piles in the kitchen dresser, where Bridget could easily reach them. She thought the three neat, fresh rooms, with their miniature modern improvements, the dearest little place to keep house in, and was continually running to Martha, who was putting up curtains in the front room, to show her something new that she had discovered. Suddenly she felt her elbow tweaked, and looking around, there stood Bridget Rafferty, the bandage gone now from her face, but still presenting the most curious appearance possible with her thin figure clad in garments of most assorted sizes and colours.

" Air them fer us? " she demanded as she took in the piles of linen, the packages of simple, wholesome groceries standing on the shelf, and the shining tin kettles that stood on the tiny range.

" Yes," said Christine.

" And the furniture, the beds, and the booro? "

" Yes," replied Christine again, but she instantly wished she had said " No," for, uttering a piercing howl, Bridget sat down, throwing her apron over her head, and burst into the loudest fit of weeping that Christine had ever heard.

Martha came quickly in to see what was the mat-

ter, and Bridget ceased as suddenly as she had commenced, wiping her eyes on her apron and smiling once
more.

"I feel better now," she said. "Yer see, we was
kinder 'shamed to send our poor sticks round to a place
like this, and I jist was thinkin' ez I came in ter do
the cleanin' how fine 'twould be ef we could hev beds
and booros and curtings, and when I saw the things
I was all took back 'twas so suddin. Couldn't help
cryin'. Mother'll cry too when she sees them, and Mick
and the baby too, I guess."

Christine wondered if the Rafferty family's one way
of enjoying themselves was having a good cry, and
Martha practically suggested that since the place was
ready they might just as well move in at once. So
Bridget departed to gather her family together and
have them in their new home for the night.

Christine was rather surprised when she went downstairs to see, instead of little Dick, whom she expected
was waiting, Teddy sitting in the pony cart while Whiskers pawed the ground as though not quite understand-
ing the change of masters.

"Dick's violin teacher wanted him to take a lesson

this afternoon," he explained, "so Aunt Georgie said I might take Whiskers out to be exercised. He is pretty fresh, for he hasn't been out for two days, and we can have a long drive, for it is only two o'clock."

Christine thought of the afternoons in Ververney when she used to drive her beloved Cherie out to the chateau, and she wished there was some place like it near Boston where they could drive on and on even though they never reached their object.

" Let's go on a pilgrimage," she said.

" A pilgrimage to what? "

" I don't know exactly, but there must be some other place besides Longfellow's house in Cambridge where we could go, we've seen that so often."

" I've just the idea," said Teddy. " Let's go out to Concord, where Miss Alcott used to live. My great-aunt Jane lives out at Lexington, and I know Concord is somewhere near there, so we'll drive out to see her and ask her the way. I know how to get to her house all right, and she'll be delighted to see us. Indeed, I ought to go, for I've only been there once since I came from abroad."

" That is just the place for us, then," Christine

14

agreed, and away they went, the frisky pony flying along at a great rate.

The snow had almost melted away and the fresh smell of the earth and the faint greenish tinge on the brown sods told of approaching spring. The country lanes bordered with bare barberry bushes seemed only waiting for a few more days to burst into leaf, and a joyous twittering and chirping told that flocks of early birds had already come up from the South to get ready their summer homes before the crowds arrived.

The children thoroughly enjoyed the fresh air and the thousand and one evidences which they could see on every hand of Nature returning to life once more. It had been a happy winter, but still they were glad that it was not winter always and that the pleasant warm days, when they could live out of doors, would soon be here. Whiskers, evidently feeling that he had gone far enough and must soon come to his journey's end, rattled fast past the broad meadows where the heroes of Lexington fell and down the broad elm-lined street which runs through the centre of the town, where Teddy pulled up before a high gabled old white house.

Teddy's great-aunt was a dear fat old lady who received them at the door all in a flutter with her cap strings flying.

"How you've grown! Ain't you hungry, my dears?" she said all in a breath, and she seated them in her cosey sitting-room that was full of old quaint furniture, and gave them each a glass of cream and some daintily-fried crullers which she assured them she had made with her own hands that morning.

After polite inquiries had been made about every one's health, Aunt Jane—for such was the dear old lady's name—noticed how Christine, quite unmindful of her good manners, let her eyes wander about the room, taking in the old pictures, the odd chairs, and peculiar old mirrors with evident interest.

"Do you like old things, my dear?" she said.

When Christine answered that she did, and confessed that the only fault that she had to find with America was that everything was so bright and new, the little lady started off on her favourite hobby. She showed them the old set of chairs that had been sent over from England for Teddy's great-great-grandmother when she was married and went to housekeeping. Her name was Priscilla, and there were quaintly painted portraits of herself and her young husband hanging over the fireplace. The old musket that he had carried through the Revolution hung over it, and Christine was glad to hear that he had gone through the war unscathed and had come home again to stay with sweet-looking Priscilla in the old house, which in their day had been new and considered wonderfully elegant.

Then Aunt Jane must show them the great punchbowl made in India and brought all the way around Cape Horn and presented to some naval officer of the family for gallant services in the War of 1812, and stores of blue china which careful housewives used to wash up themselves after breakfast.

Teddy, who was somewhat tired of hearing of his doughty ancestors and naturally had no great interest in china, now suggested that he was afraid it was time for them to be going if they had any intentions of reaching Concord that afternoon.

But Aunt Jane held up her plump hands in amazement at the proposition of the pilgrimage to Miss Alcott's house. "Bless the children," she said, "it's ten miles farther on to Concord, and you wouldn't get there before dark. Indeed, I think you had best start for home now if you don't want to give Georgiana a fright for fear of your being lost."

So they were forced to give up their adventure, though Christine did not mind much, feeling that they would get there some time, just as after so many, many attempts to reach the Chateau de Beauvoir, she had finally had such a pleasant day with Felice there.

So after many pressings to have something more to eat—for Aunt Jane seemed to feel that young people were always hungry—they prepared to return home.

"We'll come out and see you again very soon," said Teddy, "but, Auntie, as long as we've given up going to see Miss Alcott's house, tell Chris something about her. You used to know her when she was a little girl."

There evidently was some hidden teasing in this, Teddy looked so mischievous as he spoke.

The old lady shook her head at him reprovingly and said, severely, "Oh, Teddy, how can you rake up that old story?"

"You remember, Chris," answered the irrepressible Teddy, "about the story of Aunt Joe's Scrap Bag where Miss Alcott says that when she was a little girl she helped a boy cut off thirteen little pigs' tails?"

"Hush, hush!" said Aunt Jane. And then, seeing Christine's look of wonder, she added: "You see they were our pigs. Louisa grew up to be such a fine woman, but I never could quite forgive her for it."

The children shouted with laughter to think that after so many years those thirteen tails were still unforgiven. And just then, Whiskers being brought around, they kissed Aunt Jane good-bye and drove away, waving their hands to her until the house was out of sight.

They had had a delightful afternoon, and Whiskers, rested and refreshed, knew that his nose was turned homeward, and had evidently no intentions of loitering on the way.

CHAPTER XIX.

THE KING OF THE CANNIBAL ISLANDS.

"**F**RED," said little Dick one afternoon as he was lying on the sofa in the playroom, "Fred, come here." He was alone and no one could hear him, but he did not seem at all put out by that, but went right on. "You've had a good long rest, but now you're going to get pitched into, so come right here."

Fred, as you remember, was Dick's imaginary friend, and since he had had the Cremona violin which Aunt Georgie gave him at Christmas he had almost forgotten his friend and confidant, telling his joys and woes to his beloved instrument as he made sweet music upon it.

But to-day it was raining, his poor back ached, and his bones felt miserable. The other children had gone to dancing-school, and he felt quite alone and sick and forlorn.

207

For a few minutes Dick chattered away in the soft Hawaiian language which they spoke out at his home, but at last, as though the brunt of his anger had been borne, but that still he was not to be trifled with, he said sternly: "Now don't pretend you don't understand English, for I'm going to talk to you and you'd better understand." Then he lay back, and a drawn, pained look crept into his face, and although he spoke very, very low to Fred, what he said was something like this: It seems that when he had come from home in the fall he had heard such wonderful tales of the Boston doctors and all they could accomplish that he had had an idea that in a few months his back would be quite straightened out and he would be shooting up tall like Jack and Teddy. But, alas! little by little the conviction had dawned upon him that while good Dr. McIntyre was making him stronger, never, never would he be tall and straight. He had spoken no word to any one, but had nursed his hopes until he could hold them no longer, and now, as he lay there, a few bitter tears rolled down his thin cheeks and a great ache was in his heart. "I'm not going to tell any one, only you," he said bravely, " but it's been a disappointment—a terrible disappointment. It isn't that I don't have a good time, and every one loves me and is kind to me, but I should have liked to have been like other boys, and now I shall always be—just Little Dick."

Then there came into his mind the remembrance of another life where all are alike before their Maker, and the weight of sadness passed away as with simple faith he once more accepted the burden which had been given him to bear. He stretched out his hand for his violin, and when Christine came upstairs the room was flooded with sweet sounds and his face was full of contentment and peace like an angel's. The two children sat in the dark as he played, drawn closely together in their love and appreciation of all that is beautiful.

"Do you like to hear me play, Chris?" he said.

"Like it! Oh, Dick, it's wonderful!"

"And do you like me"—for the burden was still heavy to bear—"as well as though I could run around and do things for you like the boys?"

Christine's answer was to put her strong young arms around him. "Ah, Dick," she said, "there are plenty of boys who can run about and do things, but there never was another like you. We all love you so just

as you are," and so he was comforted. And indeed
Christine, for all she so regretted having no great talents, had the power of creeping into people's hearts
and of endearing herself to those about her and, what
is better yet, of keeping their affection after it was
gained. There was no more amusing instance of this
than the case of little Tommy Higgleston, whom you
will remember she had amused during the trying period
when her father was painting his portrait. He had now
emerged from his baby period into being a schoolboy.
His curls had been cut and his velvet suits given way
to rough serge, but his admiration for Christine, her
paper dolls, and her stories was unchanged. When he
met her on the street he would utter a loud yell of happiness, dashing toward her with all the speed of which his
little fat legs were capable, and now and then he would
make his appearance at the house and demand his whole
set of familiar amusements over again.

One afternoon Jack and Christine were coming
across the Common from a visit to the model lodgings
where the Raffertys were now established, when they
heard a small pathetic voice calling,

" Christine, oh, dear Christine! " and turning, there

was the usually doughty Tommy, a picture of woe.
" I'm lost," he said. " I've been lost a long time. I
ran away from Maria and I can't find her. I'm so cold
and hungry. I haven't had any lunch, and the big
policeman's keep looking at me so hard."

They comforted the little fellow, who was trying
to keep back his tears, and each holding one of his
little hands, they hurried along, for it was nearly dusk
and they felt that his mother would be terribly worried
about him.

" You can tie me with a string to Maria," sobbed
the child in his repentance when he was safe in his
mother's arms.

Mrs. Higgleston could scarcely express her thanks
to them for having brought her darling home safely and
putting an end to her anxiety. Tommy hugged Christine good-bye again and again, and then she was surprised to see him throw his arms affectionately around
Jack's neck and to hear him say:

" I'll never, never call you the King of the Cannibal
Islands again."

" What did Tommy mean by the King of the Cannibal Islands, Jack?" she asked when, tucked under her

cousin's arm, they were running home to be in time for supper.

"Oh, nothing. They just call me that at school because I came from Hawaii," he answered, rather embarrassed, and Christine, feeling that he wished the subject dropped, said no more.

But Teddy was more communicative.

"Yes," he said, "of course when Jack first came and ordered every one around so at school the boys thought he was fair sport, and they teased him until he used to nearly have fits. Fellows won't stand any nonsense you know, and he certainly had the worst of it. Lately he's been a different fellow, and they like him ever so much; but the little chaps caught on and they call him the King of the Cannibal Islands. Little Higgleston is in the primary and he must have heard it."

"How horrid boys are!" said Christine, "and Jack's so sensitive."

"Nonsense, it's all fair, Christine. Tease and tease about," answered Teddy. "Jack's really a good fellow, and the thing will soon die out as he grows popular. That's where boys have the best of things. We all have to take our teasings and keep our tempers, and Jack has been pretty game lately."

Christine felt very sorry for her cousin, but indeed she never was able to form any idea of the extent to which his class-mates had carried their teasing or the martyrdom which it had been to Jack's pride. When he opened his desk, black china dolls clad in high paper collars, labelled "Jack Learning in Native Costume," fell out. His books were adorned with caricatures of savages surrounding a kettle out of which stuck a pair of boots labelled "Missionary," and other drawings supposed to represent scenes from his former life. Conversations were arranged and carried on during recess by two or three boys concerning the habits and customs of his native land, while the rest of the class listened and applauded their sallies.

But the worst of all was a catchy song which some merry wight imported in a luckless hour for Jack. They sang it at recess, they hummed it in school hours:

> Hokus pokus, crack me crown,
> The king of the islands of knock me down
> Was thought the prettiest man in town
> When dressed in his best for a party.

Jack could never get away from it. He got into street cars and a small boy stood on the platform humming it. He went out to walk, and a mysterious sound would immediately come from somewhere near:

Satins and silks his queen did lack,
But she had some red paint that looked well upon black;
So she painted her lord and master's back
Before he set out for the party.

"Pigs and whales, and ships with sails,
And flying dragons with curly tails—
That's a thing," said she, "that never fails
To charm all the folks at a party."

When Jack appeared after his hand had been so badly burned there was a slight cessation of hostilities, and he had the good sense to see that his mates were willing to give him a fresh chance for favour, and he was not slow to take advantage of it. Before the year was out the boys sung "Hokus pokus" more in affection than derision, and in after-years, when Jack left the school for Harvard, graduating with the highest honours, when the boys had sung the school songs over and over again on the last day, a shrill young voice suddenly piped up the once hated tune and hundreds of boys' voices shouted out the verses with cheers and shouts scarcely less enthusiastic than had greeted the beloved and popular Teddy.

But this is progressing too fast, as Jack is still struggling with his unruly temper.

Christine took to heart what Teddy had said about boys' teasings, and it made her ears burn to think of the way she would have been tormented could they have seen into her mind during her infatuation for Marion, and the train of silly ideas that had filled her head at the time.

Although Christine felt after the matinée that she would never care to be friends with Marion again, Marion was so sorry, and apologized in such humble fashion to Aunt Georgie, begging to be forgiven with such contrition, that it would have taken a far harder heart than our little maiden possessed to refuse to make up.

So she went to her father's studio the days Marion posed just as before, but their friendship was never the same again. Her belief in her friend's honour and truth had been destroyed, and she could not help doubting the sincerity of the pleasant things that she was always saying. Therefore when the portrait was finished Christine was not unhappy, as she once would have been, that the opportunities for seeing Marion so frequently were over. With her schoolmates, the society of her cousins, the fun of the cooking lessons, and the sewing-circle, she was quite engrossed, and though at intervals she and Marion still met, they parted with no particular heartache on either side.

One afternoon, not many days after the finding of Tommy, the young people were assembled in the play-hall busy with their several employments, when that small gentleman arrived with a preternaturally grave countenance. He climbed up on a stiff, high chair and sat there, a ridiculous little figure with his small feet sticking straight out in front of him. He had never been known to be still for a moment before, and indeed his silence did not last long.

"What do you think the stork brought me?" he burst out.

"The stork, Tommy?"

"Yes. She brought me a baby sister. She's awfully red, but she's fine," swelling with family pride. "You should just hear her cry."

"You mustn't be so naughty any more, Tommy," said little Dick from his nest of cushions. "You'll have to set her a good example now."

"Dear me," said Tommy, sighing as though he was weighted down with the responsibility, "I don't mean to be naughty, but I do feel so wicked sometimes; it gets into my arms and legs and they will kick out, and my tongue feels so funny it just tells lies."

He looked so miserable that Christine dropped her sewing and put her arms around him to comfort him.

"If I'm better after this, Christine, don't you think I might have a piece of that nice cake with sticky chocolate on top what I had last time?" he said at last.

The cake being produced, he ate it contentedly, and then, growing restless, slid off his chair and went off to his nurse, forgetting to say good-bye.

From time to time he would come around to see Christine and report the progress of the baby, of whom he was immensely proud, and when in the course of time he grew to be a fine, manly boy with excellent control over his arms and legs and tongue, it is impossible to say how much the baby sister's influence had to do with the result.

15

CHAPTER XX.

THE HEART PARTY.

ONE morning when Christine went down to breakfast she found at her plate a large white envelope most formally addressed and sealed with a big seal. When it was opened it was found to contain an engraved card stating that she was requested to be present at a party given in honour of Marion's fifteenth birthday. In the corner of the card were the words "dancing from 7 to 11 o'clock," just as though it had been a grown folks' party.

The boys looked at the invitation admiringly, as though they thought it was very fine getting invitations to dances; and when Christine, hardly able to contain her excitement, broke out with "Oh! may I go, Auntie?" Aunt Georgie only smiled over the coffee-pot and said:

"We will talk about that later, my dear."

Christine went off to school with the invitation in her pocket and exhibited it with pride to Lily and Isabel.

"Of course you're going," said Isabel.

"I don't know," answered Christine. "Aunt Georgie may not want me to go. Indeed, I think if she did she would have told me so right away; besides, I have other reasons." For down in Christine's heart was the feeling that she did not think it was right to go to Marion's party when she had never forgotten her conduct on that eventful Saturday. She had never disclosed to any one save the family the affairs of that day, so the Nortons wondered what her other reasons could be; but she was firm, and to all their questions turned a deaf ear.

It was the afternoon of the cooking class, so Christine staid to dinner at Miss Howe's; and when the fire was burning well in the little stove the girls adjourned to the kitchen, which was only a bigger kind of playhouse to them. It had been Christine's day to purchase the marketing things, and she and Miss Howe had concocted a little plan between them.

"We thought," she said, "that it would be ever so nice to make something which could be carried to the Raffertys afterward."

Now, the last pie-crust which the little cooks had

attempted, while not so crisp and flaky as a pastry cook might desire, was still far from being uneatable, and when Miss Howe added, " I thought they might like a beefsteak-pie," three squeals of delight went up, for what so much fun as the rolling and folding, flouring and cutting of pie-crust?

It was decided to make three little pies, so every one might have a hand. Three little skillets containing the beefsteak were put on the fire, and three moulding-boards, rolling-pins, flour-sifters, and glasses of ice-water were brought out. The greatest excitement prevailed over the rolling out and the careful lining of the pie-dishes. Finally the meat was turned in, the crust put on, and the pies closed into the nice hot oven. There was quite a good deal of pastry left, and Miss Howe suggested the making of tarts, and they cut out quite a quantity with their heart-chaped cooky-cutters.

" Now if I was going to have a party," said Lily, who was extremely practical, reverting to the burning question of the morning, " I shouldn't have dancing. I'd have tarts—heart-shaped tarts—for supper. I should think one would get very sleepy dancing till eleven o'clock. I'd rather go to bed at half past eight."

Miss Howe laughed.

" I once knew some children who dressed up as the king and queen and knave of hearts," she said.

" Oh, let's do that and have tarts," cried Lily and Isabel, " only Christine couldn't come. She's going to Marion's party, so it wouldn't be any fun to have it," added Lily ruefully.

" Indeed, Lily," answered Christine, " I'm not at all sure that I shall go. I think it would be lots more fun to have a little party of our own, but I must see Aunt Georgie before I say positively."

I am not sure that the alluring prospect of dressing up as a playing-card did much to influence Christine's decision. The more she thought about it the more it seemed to her that if she was really sorry for her impatience and silly desires to be fashionable and grown up she could not show it better than by refusing this invitation, which was so exactly the fulfilment of her past day-dreams. " And if we are to have a party of our own, Marion can't be offended at my refusal," she thought.

When the pies had been taken out and cooled they were packed carefully into a basket and, little Dick and

Whiskers having been kept waiting for some time, Christine drove off with the precious basket on the seat. Bridget smiled a welcome from the door of the model lodging. It was a pleasant home, with the sunshine streaming in at the window through a nice clean muslin curtain which Christine had hemmed herself. The Raffertys were as glad to see Christine's sunny face appear as the peasant girls down at Ververney used to be, and the children looked at her and the basket with wide-open eyes of pleasure and recognition.

"We made them in our cooking class this afternoon," said Christine, disclosing the three little pies. "Our initials are in the top crust and you must tell us which one tasted the nicest. I forgot to put salt in mine, and the crust is a little burned, but I thought you'd like them all, as we made them."

Bridget raised the dishes out of the basket and set them down on the table before saying a word.

"Sure," she said, "it's a perfect party!"

The words made Christine's heart throb—"A perfect party!" It pricked her conscience to think of all the good things that she had every day of her life and how little she thought of them and valued them, and here was Bridget's little face gleaming with happiness and calling three tough-crusted pies " A perfect party." It struck a death knell at the desire for luxury and show which her acquaintance with Marion had nourished.

Dick was waiting in the street below, so Christine could not stay many minutes, but before she went she had to admire a sturdy geranium which Bridget had won by a certain number of good-conduct marks at the society of the " Little Mothers," and which was the pride of the whole household.

Christine said very little to Dick on the way home, but she went straight to Aunt Georgie, and drawing the invitation out of her pocket said:

" Auntie, I think I should rather not go to Marion's party."

" What! Not have a new dress and dance all the evening like a young lady? "

" No," said Christine, " I know it will be beautiful. I can just hear the music and see how lovely every one will look, but—I think I'll just stay at home. There'll be lots of time for grown-up parties later on."

Aunt Georgie took her in her arms.

" That's my good sensible little Christine," she said.

"We made up our minds that we would let you think about it before we influenced you in any way. Both your father and I will be very proud that our little girl has shown such good judgment."

The boys fairly howled with glee when they found Christine was not going to "the ball," as they characterized Marion's party, and they carried out Miss Howe's idea of a heart party just among themselves, which was such a success that it is doubtful whether Marion's very-much-dressed-up company had half as good a time.

In the first place, the cooking class had come out so strongly on the tarts that there would have been a great deal of excuse for the naughty knave of hearts' theft. Jack, with a gilt paper crown and stiff green and yellow paper cambric robes, sat at the head of the table; and Lily, who was certainly the best cook and of whom it could truthfully be said that "she made those tarts," sat opposite with the big plate of tarts in front of her. Teddy was the "knave," also most splendid in royal robes. Little Dick was the "ace," with a long, straight, white gown with a big heart on his chest and one on his back. Christine and Isabel were the "ten and nine," and were considered Maids of Honour. At every one's

The Royal Family of Hearts.

place was put the playing-card which they were to represent, and on the back of them Miss Howe had fastened
a piece of water-colour paper which read:

THE ROYAL FAMILY OF HEARTS.
TEA AND TARTS.

MAY 14, 189-.

The queen of hearts she made some tarts
Upon a summer's day;
The knave of hearts he stole those tarts
And took them quite away.

The Royal Family had keen appetites, and while
they were talking, sure enough, the knave stole the
tarts. The big dish suddenly and mysteriously disappeared, and in its place was only a small empty plate.

I am afraid Teddy must have had some secret un-
derstanding with Martha, who was waiting at table, for
he did not seem much perturbed, but sat looking as
contented and happy as though he had eaten every one.

Then at last, after many teasings and much looking
under the table, Teddy skipped out after Martha and
returned with the dish, and it was captured by the indignant queen, who doled them out to her subjects.
They were certainly very good and the big dish was
rapidly cleared.

Then Martha brought in another dish, but this one did not contain tarts, but three envelopes, and the girls could not understand what they were for.

"They're poems," said the king proudly. "Aunt Georgie was going to buy some decorated cards, but we said we wanted to write poems and do something for the party, so long as you made the tarts. We had a fine time writing the rhymes. There's one for each of you."

The queen opened hers and read it first, Jack growing crimson as she proceeded:

> I've stuck at this rhyme
> An awful long time,
> And my brain is on fire
> With wrath and with ire
> To think I can't write poems out of my head,
> But I guess that the best of the poets are dead.

Then Isabel read:

> Dainty and light,
> Fingers white,
> Knead and cut and bake.
> Shall it be a pie to-day?
> Or shall it be a cake?
>
> Be the bread to feed the poor,
> Or cates for my lady's table.

Spare no pains to make it light,
And do the best you are able.

Dainty and light,
Fingers white,
Knead and cut and bake.
Shall it be a pie to-day ?
Or shall it be a cake ?

It is needless to say this dainty rhyme was little Dick's. Then Christine read hers, which Teddy had written in a very different vein:

Oh, we are the Royal Famil—ee—
The king, the queen, and the little knave—ee;
We want to go and sail on the sea
  In anything that will float.

We will go in a carriage, a mousetrap, or pail,
We will start in a calm, or a breeze, or a gale,
We don't care how stout, and we don't care how **frail**,
  But we will not go out in a boat.

For the very best sailors we've heard of so far
Went to sea in a sieve in a crockery jar,
And we're bound to beat them or we'll stay where we are,
  So don't talk to us of a boat.

" Of course Aunt Georgie helped us. She started us off on the right metres, but we did most of them ourselves," said the young poets, with evident pride that if they could not make tarts, poetry was within their reach.

Then, supper being over, the Royal Family marched upstairs, and grouping around the piano, sang Mother Goose and kindred gay melodies until the big clock in the hall warned them that it was bedtime.

"Such a nice party, Aunt Georgie!" said Christine as she took off her white robe emblazoned with its nine hearts. And I do not think that she regretted at all the pomp and circumstance which she had missed by declining Marion's invitation.

You see that it was now getting well along toward summer. The trees and grass were green, and the fruit-trees had already borne and shed their fragrant masses of blossoms. The children had paid a visit to Aunt Jane in Lexington during the height of the blossom time, and had gone wild with delight over the beautiful spectacle which the old orchards presented. Miss Howe's school was to close early, and Christine was not sorry, for the warm days made her feel languid and lazy. She wished that she could transport Aunt Georgie, her father, and the boys over to the little cottage at Ververney, where her summers had always been passed, but since that was impossible for this year, she listened with contentment to Teddy's accounts of the fun they would have down by the sea, where Aunt Georgie had a roomy old homestead just suited for housing young people.

CHAPTER XXI

" A LITTLE garden now with flowers growin' in it—that was somethin' what I niver expected to see," said Bridget Rafferty, standing in the middle of the garden path and gazing with round, admiring eyes at Christine, who with a trowel was transplanting some long-stalked geraniums into a flower bed.

"You can help if you like, Bridget; indeed, you can have half the bed. We'll put some little white stones across the centre so we can tell which side belongs to you."

Bridget felt that she was in Paradise as she selected the stones from the pebbly walk and built the boundary line.

"Between the gardin and ocean, Miss Christine, this place do beat anythin'," she said, carefully digging her trowel well under the root of a geranium and depositing it in the centre of the bed.

230

Gray Marshes, while it may not have beaten everything, was certainly a delightful place for the summer
vacation. Close to the rock-bound Cape Cod coast,
where the ocean roared and surged, Aunt Georgie's old
Puritan ancestors had built their low-lying comfortable
homestead. The well-seasoned timbers had withstood
the sea storms of more than a hundred years, and the
weather-beaten house, with its old-fashioned garden laid
out in box-bordered beds of foxglove, clove pinks, and
sweet Williams, was a veritable happy playground for
the young people. With the warm summer weather
that comes so suddenly upon the dwellers in cities Aunt
Georgie had noticed that Christine's cheeks grew pale
and that Dick lay languidly for many hours among his
pillows. So leaving Jack with Mrs. Hubbard for the
few weeks that remained of his school term, she came
down to Gray Marshes with Dick and Christine.

Christine had never been at the seashore before, and
Dick, who only knew the soft tropical shores of his
native land, was delighted with the strong rugged type
of the rock-bound coast. They drove Whiskers up and
down on the hard beach, they splashed about in the
water, Cap'n Lewis took them out in his big schooner

to the lobster pots, and their cheeks grew rosy and brown in the strengthening salt air.

Little Dick was radiantly happy. For two weeks he had his dear cousin all to himself, and when he grew tired of running about with her or she worked in her garden he would curl himself up in one of the broad window seats and, looking out at the bit of the ocean which could be seen through an opening in the garden trees, his hands would noiselessly draw the bow over the old Cremona as though he was trying to catch the mysterious melody of the ocean's voice.

But there was one person still more contented, and that was Bridget Rafferty. She had been ailing, and Aunt Georgie had provided some one to look after the babies for a couple of weeks and brought her down to Gray Marshes. It was all so new to her—the flowers, the trees, the water—after the dingy rear tenement in which almost all her life had been passed, it seemed too good to be real. She helped the gardener weed the flower beds, she shelled the peas, and ran countless errands for every one.

"When we're grown up," Christine said to her one day when she found her at work on one of the tasks that were her idea of playing, "and I keep house for father, you must come and be my maid."

From that time on Bridget had an ideal, a dream for which she lived—it was to be Christine's maid.

The days flew by quickly and it did not seem as though three weeks could possibly have passed when Mr. and Mrs. Hubbard came down to their place, which was not very far away on the sea road, and with them came Jack and Teddy, feeling very manly in the consciousness of examinations passed creditably.

With their arrival the trim cat-boat, The Owl and the Pussy Cat, which was painted a beautiful pea-green to carry out the legend, was put into sailing order. With Dick and Christine for passengers, the boys took many long sails up and down the coast, their strong young arms being quite equal to the reefing and furling of the sails.

The Columbian Fair was now opened in Chicago, but it had been decided that the young people should go out in September, when the weather was cool.

Christine had never quite forgiven the Fair for having separated her so many months from her dear father, but she felt that things were somewhat equalized when

16

she found that among the many foreigners whom the exhibition attracted to this country, who should be coming but her little French friend Felice, whom you will remember when Christine was living at the cottage in Ververney. The two girls had written to each other all winter, Christine in French, Felice in strangely constructed English sentences. Christine knew all about the convent, and she had kept Felice informed about her cousins, the Nortons, and all the events of the winter.

When Aunt Georgie learned that the Count and Countess de Beauvoir were coming to this country she sent them a kindly worded invitation in case they should come to Boston, and what was Christine's delight to find that, their engagements requiring them to visit an old relative in Brookline, they would gladly let Felice go to Gray Marshes for a week.

The boys groaned unanimously at the prospect of a French girl—all nerves and chatter. They would take to the water—they would never speak to her. They vowed it again and again.

When Felice came she was most terribly homesick. Her big brown eyes were so wistful and sad that she was quite pathetic to behold, and her pretty broken-English sentences were uttered in a low voice that could scarcely be called chattering. She clung to Christine as a link which bound her to her native land, and was so evidently miserable that the boys laid their heads together to devise all manner of ways of cheering her.

Now it was that Jack, the once gruff and grumpy, came to the rescue in a manner wonderful to behold. Clever as he was in his studies, he was a most indifferent linguist, and the first smile that came to Felice's face was raised by the extraordinary sentences which he proudly considered French conversation. Under her polite criticism he felt he was improving wonderfully. They soon got to be friends, and Felice in English and Jack in French carried on long talks which certainly, if they could understand each other, were all that could be desired.

Felice would say:

" Ze ship you go her ze après, après after, after-noon."

And Jack would reply:

" Oui, à trois o'clock, o'clock, heures; merci, made-moiselle, à trois heures, vous aussi come."

Then Felice would smile, showing all her pretty, even teeth, and would be sure to join the party at three o'clock.

" This is better than being at Ververney with Jeanneton," she said one day to Christine when her homesickness had worn off and she was once more her lively self, telling tales of her escapades at the convent, her intolerance of being watched, and her desire to be brought up *à l'Anglais*.

" You boat, you swim, you go about with your cousins all the day. Oh, cousins are so stiff in France! They are no good. I think America must be the place for little girls."

" I think so too," answered Christine. " I'm sure it's the place for me, though I was awfully homesick at first. But come; there's Teddy hoisting the sail on The Owl and the Pussy Cat. We must hurry up or we'll be late for the picnic."

" The peck-neck? Let us run," cried Felice, and the two girls flew along the sand to the place where the boat lay with its white sails gleaming in the sun, all ready to take them out to Captain Johnson's Cave, a romantic spot some miles up the coast which boasted a cave which was supposed to have been used by Captain Johnson during the Revolution as a storehouse for firearms and ammunition.

The young people were to have supper in the open air, and Aunt Georgie and Mrs. Hubbard, with plenteous baskets of provisions, accompanied the little boat in Frank's yacht. On the way out Teddy, who knew every stick and stone of the coast and all the legends of wrecks and treasure-trove, beguiled the time with a real true story of how in the Revolution the British soldiers had discovered Captain Johnson's hiding-place and were going to make a raid, when he got wind of their coming. It seems that it was not always muskets and gunpowder that were concealed there. On this occasion he had a large amount of Spanish gold sent by private sympathizers with the rebellious colonies.

There was no time to bury the money, so the sturdy sailor dropped it down into the cave and was shot by the soldiers who had been balked of their game.

What boy's heart does not bound with thoughts of secret treasures? Even Christine and Felice were filled with a desire to explore the cave.

"Teddy," said Christine when they had finished their supper, " I want to go down in the cave."

" Nonsense! " said Teddy. " You're afraid of lobsters; you'd have a fit if you went down in the cave. Why, we might meet a sea serpent."

But Aunt Georgie pooh-poohed the idea of the girls being afraid when the boys were ready for the expedition.

" I've been down any number of times," she said, " and I don't think there is the least danger of a sea serpent or anything else frightening the girls."

So Christine and Felice joyously set off with Jack and Teddy, who carried the ship's lantern. They picked their way gingerly over the stones at the mouth of the cave, leaping from stone to stone, the vault echoing with their voices, and finally found themselves in shallow water.

Whether the tide was remarkably low, or whether no one happened to go there when the tide was so far out, I do not know, but the end of the cave was almost dry, and Felice, slipping with her wet shoes off a big stone on to the sand, dug her hands into it to save herself from falling. When she stood up laughing, her hands full of sand, she had clutched a stone—no, not a stone, it was a big tarnished coin—an old Spanish dollar.

Teddy gave a loud whoop of joy as he examined it under the light of the lantern. It was the long-buried treasure he was sure. The children searched and dug, but no more coins were discovered, and finally they noticed the tide creeping in and were forced to abandon their search.

They rushed to Aunt Georgie, all talking at once, and exhibited the treasure, Felice as delighted as possible at the adventure. The boys were planning schemes for digging up the entire cave and most of the bay, when Aunt Georgie, who had been turning the coin over, interrupted them.

" Why, dears," she said, " this isn't one of Captain Johnson's coins. See, it has a hole in it. I remember this quite well. My father wore it on his watch-chain for many years; indeed, he was quite provoked when he lost it one day when he took us into the cave when I was about twelve years old."

So the golden dreams of a cave full of gold had to be abandoned, though it seemed nearly as interesting as finding the treasure to find a pocket-piece after so many years.

There was a stiff breeze blowing on the sail home, and as the tired mariners tumbled into their beds they declared there had never been such an interesting day.

As for the coin, duly polished it was presented to Felice, who always kept it as a souvenir of her American visit.

CHAPTER XXII

SOMETHING of Captain Johnson's brave spirit must have lingered about the scene of his gallant defence and death, for after the visit to the cave and the finding of the Spanish dollar the young people at Gray Marshes broke out into a tremendous fever of patriotism. There was a great getting out of histories and telling of revolutionary tales, and the only drawback seemed to be that Aunt Georgie, who could tell such interesting stories of the civil war, had had no personal experience of the Revolution.

Although Christine had studied an outline of American history, she found that it was very different from the stories Aunt Georgie read of Washington's courage and heroism, of the stout farmers who fought at Lexington, of the brave hearts who never gave up in the long struggle, and the wise heads who held to the cause of freedom through every temptation. Washington,

241

whom she had formerly associated with being on a postage-stamp, grew to be a hero.

"We helped you too," said Felice one day when they were reading about the Marquis de La Fayette; and indeed she had come to love this country almost as ardently as her illustrious countryman.

"Yes, you helped," said Aunt Georgie, smiling into her beaming face. "The only thing is, children, you mustn't think the struggle as all over yet. You all have work to do. Being good citizens and helping make and keep good laws is just as much a noble thing as fighting."

"Well," said Teddy, "I'm sure I should like to have been a general—not Washington, but one of the dashing ones—or——"

"I'd rather have been Nathan Hale," said little Dick.

"Nathan Hale! Why, he was captured and killed."

"Yes, I know, but I like him best; I think he was noble," answered little Dick, who had learned in his short suffering life that the battle is not always to the strong and that the greatest success does not always make the greatest hero.

"Christine and I," said Felice, "would have staid at home and spun or we would have helped on the soldiers if there was a battle near. My ancestress, the Marquise de La Valjen, kept her castle against the English for days and days until the French army came up. She is my favourite grandmother, and her portrait hangs in the gallery at the chateau."

Felice's eyes glistened and her cheeks were bright, as though she would like nothing better than to imitate her heroic ancestor.

But Christine said nothing. She was thinking deeply of what Aunt Georgie had said about the struggle not yet being over, and that one must be a good citizen.

"Teddy," she said the next day, when they were scudding along with a good wind in The Owl and the Pussy Cat, "are girls American citizens too?"

Teddy stopped for a moment in reefing the sail.

"Christine," he said, "what have you got in your head? You're not going to be strong-minded and want to vote, are you?"

"Why, no, Teddy, only I was wondering——"

"Well, Chris, I shouldn't wonder. Men," drawing

himself up proudly, "attend to all those questions. Father and Frank talk politics by the hour and mother sits by and listens. Now and then she puts in a word, but not often."

"Very well, Teddy, if when I'm a woman you let me put in a word now and then I shall be satisfied, only I hope I shall know what you're talking about, even if I am a girl."

"Oh, Chris, you've forgotten the centreboard," cried the citizen reproachfully, and sure enough she had, in the interest of the conversation, and the little boat was most unhappily aground on a sand bank.

It was hopelessly stuck and, worst of all, they were in one of the narrow channels of the salt marshes where the high weeds on either side of the inlet shut them out from sight. They sat ruefully in the bottom of the boat, prepared for several hours' martyrdom before the tide should float them off. Suddenly they heard a cheerful voice coming from behind the reeds.

"Stuck, be ye?"

"Oh, Captain Jansen," they cried, recognising the voice of the ancient lobster and clam man, "do you think you can get us off?"

The ragged sail of his ancient dory appeared around the corner of the reeds.

" Well, I dew declar'," he said, " howiver did yer git stuck ? "

" We were talking politics," said Teddy, who had known the old salt for many years and knew he would enjoy the joke.

" Talkin' politics! Well, I never! " he roared out with a jolly laugh. " Well, just hitch yerselfs inter my boat and I guess I can float yers off."

Float them off he did with the aid of pulls and tugs, and when they were safely under weigh again they could still hear him roaring with laughter and ejaculating, " Talkin' politics! "

Christine felt that her first discussion had not been a success, and she devoted herself entirely to the centreboard and to ducking her head when the boom swung around, until they were safely out of the marshes in the wide bay.

But it would seem as though the afternoon had been decreed by Fate to be an eventful one, for late toward dusk, as they were scudding back, just as they neared the marshes a sudden gust of wind and an unwise tacking of the small sail brought the little craft over on its side. As it went over, Christine happily caught hold of the side and, with but small wetting, climbed on to the upturned keel; but Teddy, thrown completely overboard by the sudden collapse, was wet to the skin. It was too far to swim to land, and the boat was too heavy for him to tow if he could have kept on for such a distance. At last he succeeded in climbing up beside Christine, his clothes dripping with water and presenting a very drowned-puppy appearance. By this time it was quite dark, and they were filled with anxiety at the thought of spending the night on the upturned keel of the boat like mud turtles squatted on a rock. The slow lapping of the waves as they drifted with the tide and the strange helplessness of being there among so much water made their hearts sink, though they tried to maintain a cheerful demeanour toward each other and to treat it as a great lark. They screamed and shouted to attract attention, but no one seemed moving on the dim shore and the water was perfectly still—not the sound of an oar or the flap of a sail. They were, oh, so hungry and cold! and the fog settling down took all the ardour out of their spirits, and they clung together for warmth and comfort in the middle of their uncomfortable craft. When they had given up all hope and Teddy was trying to keep up Christine's courage to passing the night drifting about in the bay, they suddenly saw a light approaching through the gloom, and a familiar voice shouted:

" Stranded, be ye! Lork's upsot—clean upsot," and there again was the friendly clam man, his red face and bushy whiskers appearing in the radius of light.

" Talking politics ag'in, was yer!" he kept muttering as he steadied the wobbling cat-boat and helped the stiff and tired pair into his dory. Away they scudded with the upturned boat in tow, and before many minutes were safe in their respective homes, being put to bed and fed with hot drinks to prevent any bad consequences from the exposure and wet. Happily enough, neither of them suffered in the least from their ducking, and for many days they kept the household in roars of laughter describing their mud-turtley situation and the sudden appearance of the ancient clam man with his lantern, peering through the mist like the Dong with the Luminous Nose. And whenever they met that ancient worthy sitting on the sand or sailing his boat, they would always be greeted by a roar of laughter and a chuckle, "Talkin' politics, be ye?" as though their conversation had been the one joke which had ever percolated through Captain Jansen's brain.

They happily had no more adventures of the kind, and the cat-boat remained " right side up with care " for the rest of the summer. But every day was not pleasant and sunshiny so they could be out on the water, and the first rainy day was rather hailed with delight, since they could do many little things which had been neglected in the constant enjoyment of outdoor sports.

There was a trunk of old costumes in the attic, and since the history readings had been inaugurated Aunt Georgie had intended to get them down, but the matter had been delayed until this very afternoon, when she thought looking over them would be just the thing for the children's amusement. So the trunk was brought down and opened with a big old hand-wrought key, and its contents, laid away in linen wrappings and scented with old lavender, were taken out.

They crowded about, examining each parcel, and exclaiming over the quaintness of the old coats, and cocked hats, and the stiff brocaded gowns that the Puritan belles had worn year after year at the Governor's balls.

Down in the bottom of the trunk there was a simple gray homespun gown, and Aunt Georgie said that, so the story went, her great-grandmother had woven the stuff with her own hands and worn it for her wedding gown during the hard days of the Revolution.

"Let's dress up," said Felice, true little Frenchwoman to her finger tips, who longed to array herself in the old silken finery. So the boys picked out knee-breeches, and flowered waist-coats, and tail coats, and Felice found it hard to decide between a short-waisted white wedding dress and a gorgeous brocade, deciding at last for the brocade.

But Christine would have none of these. When the boys with their powdered heads came laughing into the room, feeling very fine in their bravery, albeit it was several sizes too big and not guiltless of pins, Felice, a perfect Dresden-china marquise in her gorgeousness, with her high hair powdered and a coquettish patch on her pretty cheek, rose and made a stately court courtesy, smiling over her big fan.

17

"Where's Christine?" cried little Dick from his favourite seat by the window.

And then Christine came down the old oak stairs, a veritable picture of the fair-haired wife of the builder of the house in the old homespun gown, with a white kerchief around her neck and her long braid turned up and concealed by a little muslin cap.

The boys clapped their hands at the pretty picture and executed their best court bows, and Mr. Averil, Aunt Georgie, and little Dick could not sufficiently admire the gay group.

Then Aunt Georgie played the opening bars of the court quadrille which they had all learned at dancing-school, and they went through the stately dance with such airs and graces, such posturings and deep reverence, as would not have disgraced their ancestors themselves.

Indeed, it may be said that the Puritan lady was in no way outdone by the fine marquise, and Teddy her partner quite decided that, for all the freckles on her nose, Christine was a mighty nice looking girl.

The next day Felice had to go back to Boston to meet her parents, and great was the sorrow at parting from her. The boys, who had dreaded her coming, had grown to consider her one of themselves, and Christine was only consoled for her loss by the prospect of seeing her later in Chicago.

So the summer days flew by at Gray Marshes— happy, happy days. And when the autumn came it was a rosy-cheeked, hearty little maiden who went out to the Fair and had a fine time there among all the wonderful sights, as the boy or girl who is reading this book probably did.

When they came back from their journey and Christine was settled once more in the house in Mount Vernon Street she was surprised one afternoon to have Aunt Georgie come up to the big playroom and ask Teddy to stay to tea.

" We're going to have a little celebration—nothing much, only an extra good cake; but I thought you would like to stay," she said.

" Why, is it some one's birthday?" asked Jack.

" No, not a birthday. Don't you remember what day it is, Christine?"

" No, Auntie."

" Why, it's just a year ago to-day that we landed."

"A year! a whole year, Auntie? Why, it only seems yesterday. I can't believe it."

"Yes, dear, it really is," said Aunt Georgie, smiling. "And it shows that it has been a happy one if it has passed so quickly."

Jack and Teddy looked up from their work and little Dick from his cushions.

"It has been a happy year for all of us," they said.

CHAPTER XXIII.

SWEET SEVENTEEN.—CONCLUSION.

S O the years rolled by over Christine's sunny head—four long, happy years well spent with her studies, her playmates, her cousins, and the many interests which had grown about her life.

"Sweet seventeen!" What a big girl she feels as she rises on her birthday morning! Before she is dressed in comes Aunt Georgie in her dressing-gown to give her seventeen kisses and a beautiful gift—a gold hairpin such as young ladies wear in their hair. Then Christine realizes that she is old enough to wear her hair put up, and indeed she is so big and her dresses so long that this coiling up of her hair only adds to her sweet womanly look.

Aunt Georgie brushes the waving mass—which is beautiful despite Teddy's epithet of red, which he would never think of applying now—up from her white neck and coils it around her head in grown-up fashion with the pin stuck in the top.

Christine looks at herself in the glass and is half laughing, half crying, to see how much of a young lady she is.

" I don't want to be anything but your dear girl, Auntie," she says, but she does not take the pin out.

Then Mr. Averil must admire the new coiffure, and Dick seems quite in awe of his tall young cousin when she comes down to breakfast with her head carried very high in its new dignity and the gold hairpin gleaming among her ruddy locks. She has to go to school soon, so the hairpin is taken out and put in its white box, and she sets off to Miss Howe's with a light heart and with a letter of congratulaiton from Felice—whose father is dead and who is now the Countess Beauvoir—in her pocket.

The school is just the same, the Norton girls just as good companions, and they still cook in the little kitchen, though lately they have not been concocting leathery beefsteak pies.

There is an afternoon session now, and Christine is very much interested, I can assure you, in some of

those very "ologies" which frightened her so at first
at Miss Baldwin's. But take her all in all, she is not a
very booky girl, though she likes to read the books and
poems that are classics in English, French, and German,
and Miss Howe has proved a kindly mentor in helping
her to choose and discriminate.

When Christine got home from school she went
straight to her room and changed her dress, putting on
a pretty, soft terra-cotta that suited her complexion very
well, and which, if not so " fashionable " as the gowns
she used to envy Marion, was certainly quite as pretty.
As she looked at herself again in the glass, half ashamed
of her vanity in once more wishing to admire her grown-
up coil with the beautiful hairpin in it, Martha knocked
on the door and handed in on a little silver tray a visiting card.

" Who," thought Christine, " can be coming to call
on me so formally?" and her surprise was increased
when she read the card,

> "THEODORE CABOT HUBBARD,
>
> "*Mount Vernon Street.*"

" Why, it's Teddy! " she said, seeing Martha smile.

" Yes, miss, it's Mister Teddy," said Martha, who had called the boy Master Teddy from his birth.

Sure enough, of course it was Teddy sitting in the drawing-room under the picture of the bay of Honolulu —such a big nineteen-year-old Teddy that his friends were afraid he would never stop growing until he was so big that he wouldn't be able to get through the doors.

" Why, what a young lady you are! " said Teddy teasingly. " I heard all about the turned-up hair from Dick this morning. He stopped in with his fiddle on the way to the Conservatory, so I thought you might expect me to come and call with a card. I half fancied you would send down word that you were out."

" Oh, Teddy, you didn't."

" Yes, indeed, I did."

" Teddy, come up to the playroom and sit on the old sofa. You look so grown up sitting in that chair with that depressing picture of the bay of Honolulu hanging over you that I can't think of anything to talk about except the weather."

" Do you remember how we thought Dick and Jack would be black? "

" Yes; I was terribly disappointed, and I think you were."

" So you don't want really to be considered grown up, Christine, and have formal calls and have compliments paid you—you're going right on——"

" Being your little sister, yes, Teddy."

" Very well, Christine, let's go upstairs to the hall. I grieve that I have wasted upon you my very, very highest collar, but I thought the occasion demanded it." For Teddy was much of a dude and sported the very highest of high collars in these days.

When they were comfortably settled in the dilapidated old chairs in the square hall which had been the scene of so many useful and happy hours, Teddy, after much teasing and wondering and boyish " what will you give to know?" which strung Christine's anxiety up to a high pitch, imparted the news that in another month he was going to Paris to take the examinations for entering the Beaux Arts. His boyish dream of wishing to be an architect was to be fulfilled. He had been studying in an architect's office all winter, and it had been decided that he showed sufficient ability to warrant the foreign training.

Christine knew how much his heart had been set upon it, and she could only say:

"Oh, I'm so glad for you!" but she had a sharp pang at heart that her old playmate was going away.

But she entered into all Teddy's plans and hopes with warm sympathy, and often in his lonely lodgings in Paris the boy remembered it and longed for a good talk with her when he was homesick and discouraged over his work.

"Teddy, you must study so hard," said Christine, "and get to be a great architect so that your name will be written up on the wall as father's is. I shall never forget how proud I was when I saw it there. I used to make myself so unhappy when I was a little girl because I wasn't talented like mamma and papa. Do you remember telling me on the steamer that I was so homely you supposed I was clever. I couldn't forget it."

"Oh, dear," said Teddy, "did I say that? What an awful youngster I must have been!"

"Yes, it made me very wretched. My career was always bothering me, but somehow since I've lived with Aunt Georgie I've learned to be contented. You and Jack and Dick are all going out in the world to do so much, but I'm glad that I am going to stay at home with father and Auntie and always be——"

" Our dear little Chris."

Our dear little Chris! Could anything more be said, for though our heroine will never paint pictures, carve statues, or write verses, she has the sweet womanly qualities of thoughtfulness, kindness, and sweetness that attaches all those with whom she comes in contact.

They talk of their meeting in Paris so long ago, reviewing past escapades and long-forgotten pranks. Dick, coming in with his violin under his arm from one of his " Happy Hours "—for he still is a ray of sunshine to the little crippled children—hears their merry laughter and bounds upstairs to warn them that it is time to dress for dinner. Yet he can not resist just a few minutes' chat, and curls up on the end of the sofa beside Christine.

" Are you tired, Dick, dear? " she says, smiling.

" No, Christine, I'm never tired now," for Dick, though he is not very big, is quite well and strong owing to Dr. McIntyre's wonderful care. " Going to Paris! Oh, Teddy, how fine! I shall come over with the fiddle some time and ring at the Beaux Arts gates, 'Where, oh, where is our jolly Teddy?' and you will come out with a fierce pair of black mustachios and an enormous compass in your hand and cry 'Begone! I only talk in French.'"

"No, I won't. I shall say, 'Is that the voice of Richard the Knight of Hawaii? Tune up, my friend, and give us Annie Rooney.'"

This ditty being still the favourite of the hospital children, Dick thinks that he must have been listening.

So they sit in the dark and make plans for all going over to France in Teddy's vacations—for the doctor has forbidden Dick's returning to the enervating climate of Hawaii—of the trips they will take together, and how they will see all the beautiful pictures that are in Mr. Averil's photograph albums. They talk of vacations at Gray Marshes, of the heart and tart party, of the Lady of the Lake, of Felice—of everything they can think of until Martha, with small respect now for visiting cards and dressed hair, comes up with a sharp "Master Teddy, Miss Georgie says you have got to go home to dress."

For Christine is to have a little dinner party, just her own little circle of friends, but a dinner party instead of the tea parties of bygone years.

When she is dressed in her pretty fluffy white gown she runs into her aunt's room to see the effect in the long pier glass, and can scarcely believe that such a beautiful reflection is her own. Lily and Isabel come muffled up in long cloaks, and Marion, who is very much of a young lady and somewhat bored and languid after a winter's dissipation, for she is " out " now.

They all march into the dining-room where they had the heart party and many other jollifications, and through their soup every one is quite stiff and correct and they talk quite as stupidly as most grown-up people do under the same circumstances.

Then tongues are loosened. The football match is fought up and down the table. The affairs of Harvard, where Jack is now an uproarious freshman, come in for their share of interest, and the girls all envy Marion, who is going to " Class Day."

At last the birthday cake is brought in with its seventeen blazing candles—a beautiful light cake frosted and decorated by whose skilful fingers do you suppose but Bridget Rafferty's, who is still in training to be Miss Christine's own maid.

A triumphant shout goes up when Teddy gets the ring, having nearly swallowed it for a raisin. Then they rise from the table and, singing some of Jack's college catches, group themselves around Aunt Georgie at the piano and sing until the roof rings.

Then little Dick must have out his violin—the old Cremona that was Ole Bull's and which has been his dearest friend since the Christmas night when it came to be his.

First he plays all the old favourites—beautiful music that touches Aunt Georgie, that makes languid Marion think of other things beside her new ball dress, that brings a throb into Teddy's honest heart, and makes Jack remember that his college life isn't all fun.

Then he plays a new air, a little sad air of parting, of separation—the very thought that has been echoing in Christine's heart during these last months of her school days.

But the minor chords change to joyousness, to a song of life and light, of the fruition of the good seed that has been sown.

So with the soft strains of the melody echoing in her ears we will leave Christine standing on the threshold of her new life, a sweet prophecy of the happiness that will come in her career of loving, thoughtful womanhood.

THE END.

www.ingramcontent.com/pod-product-compliance
Lightning Source LLC
Chambersburg PA
CBHW021044030726
47496CB00006B/1674